A bride without a groom

"Don't worry—there won't be any more scenes like this morning. So we'll just stay friends—and enjoy our 'honeymoon' together. How does that sound?"

"Oh, wonderful." But if he heard the savage sarcasm with which she invested the word, Jake gave no sign.

She had been almost reconciled to this unstoppable man's hijacking her honeymoon. *A honeymoon is a game for two players....* There was some truth in that, although not in the way Jake had meant it. She had no intention of playing that kind of game, and she had planned to make that perfectly clear.

So why did she find it so infuriating that Jake Farrell had been the one to change the rules?

ELEANOR REES lives on the very edge of a little Chilterns town with the man who is the model for all her heroes—or so she tells him—and two cats. The cats, she says, approve of her writing as it keeps her lap stationary for long periods of time. Plus, they make their own contribution by strolling up and down the computer keyboard when Eleanor isn't looking. Her ambition is to write full-time and to live in the sort of place that gets snowbound in the winter. "I can't think of anything more romantic," she says.

Books by Eleanor Rees

HARLEQUIN PRESENTS
1285—THE SEAL WIFE
1452—PIRATE'S HOSTAGE

ELEANOR REES

Hijacked Honeymoon

Harlequin Books

TORONTO • NEW YORK • LONDON
AMSTERDAM • PARIS • SYDNEY • HAMBURG
STOCKHOLM • ATHENS • TOKYO • MILAN
MADRID • WARSAW • BUDAPEST • AUCKLAND

ISBN 0-373-11645-4

HIJACKED HONEYMOON

CHAPTER ONE

'STOP! Oh, please stop!' Down in the village, Amber could hear the church clock strike midnight. Only thirty-nine hours to go before her wedding... But at that moment there was room in her brain for only one worry—that, if she didn't get out of the stuffy little minicab she was sharing with what seemed like half the female population of Marchings, she was going to faint. Or be spectacularly car-sick. Or possibly—probably—both.

Fortunately the driver understood her clenched-teeth mumblings and the car screeched to an urgent halt by the roadside. Amber stumbled out, gulping the cool, fresh air in huge draughts, and felt the nausea gradually recede. Behind her, as if in another existence, she could hear the ribald comments of her colleagues from the travel agency, made uncharacteristically boisterous by the drink they had consumed.

'Come on, love—can't waste your beauty sleep, you know.' That was May, whose revelations about her own marriage as the evening progressed had made Amber wonder if she would ever be able to look the woman's quiet little husband in the face again. 'You've only two nights left as Amber Ashley. And tomorrow night you won't be able to sleep——'

'And the night after that, Amber *Farrell* won't want to!' another voice cut in. Beverley, at eighteen, was five years Amber's junior but already possessed more bouncy self-confidence than she would ever have. Especially with men... 'How long's the honeymoon? This could be your last chance to sleep for the next four weeks!'

The two of them dissolved into giggles. They meant well enough, Amber knew, but their drunken good humour sparked off in her a sudden distaste. She wasn't ready yet to think of her marriage to Simon on quite such an earthy level.

But if not yet, then when? a voice inside her seemed to query. They had been engaged for almost three years—and even before that she could hardly remember a time when she hadn't assumed that she and her cousin would marry. They had grown up together. But now the waiting was almost over...

Her hands tightened in sudden panic and she felt the stones of her engagement ring cutting into her palm. The pounds she had lost in the last few months had left it loose and insecure, and the weight of the diamonds in their heavy antique setting kept pulling it round. With nervous fingers, she twisted it back, realising guiltily that, once again, she had forgotten to take it in for alteration, and that it was now almost certainly too late to have it done before the wedding.

Simon would be angry—twice recently the ring had slipped off and she had nearly lost it. She had promised to remember. But somehow she had felt oddly reluctant, and the task had kept slipping her mind. As if a part of her had wanted to be free of the ring's cumbersome weight . . .

The worries that she had been trying to suppress came rushing back in on her, swamping her, and Amber felt the sick feeling rise again in her throat. In less than two days' time it would have happened. She would be lying in his arms, and there would be no more excuses about waiting until they were married to save her——

Save her? What was she thinking of? She would be Simon's wife . . . And it wasn't as if either of them would be expecting the sort of passion that belonged between the covers of one of the novels Beverley was so fond of reading. Amber had watched her mother spend her life restlessly searching for that kind of passion, and she knew only too well how empty and transient it could be. How cruel . . .

She felt the tears come, and blinked them back. No. Theirs would be different—a civilised marriage. She and Simon were fond of each other. Everything would be all right. It was only natural to be nervous. Everyone said so——

'Amber, are you OK?' This time, there was real concern in the voice that broke into her thoughts. But that was typical of Sandra, the only one of her companions she would really have counted as a friend. She had known her as long as she had known Simon. Ever since as children, they had all played together; the two cousins from the Hall and Sandra Atkins, the housekeeper's daughter. Aunt Bella had discouraged friendships 'in the village', but made an exception in her case. And Sandra, two years older than

Amber, had taken the shy little girl under her protective wing.

And now, almost ten years later, she was still looking after her. It had been Sandra who had offered a bed for the night, knowing that Amber would hardly enjoy her 'hen' party if she had to go back to the censorious comments of her aunt and future mother-in-law, Mrs Farrell. And it had been Sandra, too, who had been sensitive enough to see that the evening was becoming too much for the guest of honour and had persuaded the others to leave the club at what had seemed to them a ridiculously early hour.

'Yes—just car-sick.' Another wave of faintness threatened, and Amber steadied herself against the still-open door of the cab. 'And too much to drink, I suppose.' Although in reality she knew she had drunk very little, mindful of the long list of tasks that Aunt Bella would be expecting her help with next day. But it was an excuse that her tipsy companions would readily accept. And it was true enough that the few glasses of wine she had consumed seemed to be having a disproportionate effect. She felt strangely exhilarated...

'I think I'd better walk the rest of the way.' The mere thought of getting back into the car was enough to make her feel queasy again.

There was a chorus of protest from the back seat, but the cabbie came in firmly on her side. 'It's only five minutes from here. She'll be fine.' No doubt he believed she was drunk and was just worried about his upholstery, but Amber was grateful for his support.

'Then I'll come with you.' Sandra, trapped between the other two women, started to scramble towards the door.

'No, honestly.' From somewhere, Amber summoned up a smile. Suddenly she wanted to be alone; to think things out... Her brain was muzzy with tiredness, and yet somehow she felt that, if only she could concentrate, she might see things more clearly in the cool darkness than in the bright light of day. 'Please, Sandra, I'd rather you didn't. And don't wait up for me; I think I might go home after all. It's nearer, for one thing. And Aunt Bella will have gone to bed by now, as she's not expecting me.'

'Well, if you're sure...' Sandra dithered, but the other two, their tipsy cheerfulness now cooling into sleep, backed Amber up. And at last the taxi pulled away, leaving her standing alone in the moonlight.

As the noise of the cab died away, Amber felt a weight lift from her spirits. She was alone at last... And she was free! Her feeling of relief took her aback. Had she really been so trapped, then, these last few months?

It was true that she never felt alone; that since the end of her college course she and her cousin had been swept along on a tide of preparations that seemed to have a momentum all of its own. And it was true, too, that Mrs Farrell's constant references to grandchildren were beginning to wear her down.

As a child, Amber had found her aunt's preoccupation with what was always referred to portentously as 'The Family' a source of amusement. And Bella Farrell did have reason for her pride in its achievements. Her father's firm had become almost synonymous with travel agency, and the shops bearing Matthew Farrell's name were to be found on every high street.

But, since her son and niece had announced their engagement, this preoccupation had developed into an obsession—and Amber had found herself in the front line. Despite the fact that Amber had just spent three years working for a degree in 'Languages and Tourism' with a view to entering the family business, Aunt Bella had fought hard against her taking her present job, claiming that, since her niece would soon be giving it up to be a mother, there was little point starting a career.

But there Amber had put her foot down. It wasn't that she needed the money—her grandfather's will had provided her with an income more than adequate for her needs. But some puritanical streak in her make-up had rebelled against living off the profits of a business to which she had contributed nothing. So she had applied for the company's management trainee scheme, and won a place, she hoped, on her own merits.

She twisted the ring on her finger as she remembered how angry Aunt Bella had been, then sharply pulled her hand away, irritated by what was becoming a nervous habit. And unfortunately Simon had backed his mother up. But, as Amber had tried to explain, it wasn't that she didn't want children. She did; and when they arrived she would be delighted. She just wished it weren't all happening so fast...

She shook her head to try and clear the thoughts that buzzed confusedly round in her brain. She ought to go back. No doubt all brides felt like this. The others had been right—she needed to sleep... And yet the idea of going back to the Hall, of creeping obediently up the stairs to her bedroom and slipping sensibly into her narrow bed, made her shudder with claustrophobic horror.

Free at last... The rebel note sounded again in her head as she felt her steps turning, almost against her will, up the path to the woods. Towards her thinking-place. That thought surprised her too—how long was it since she had remembered her childish bolt-hole? Too long, the rebel voice answered. Seven, eight years? Amber tried for a moment to remember when she had stopped coming. It seemed important. But the memories eluded her like moths in the darkness.

She stumbled on the soft, muddy path and kicked off the high-heeled, elegant shoes she had worn for the party, picking them up to carry them in her hands. The ground was cool under her feet.

Amber felt her resolution harden. She would go to her thinking-place. And then she would know what to do.

She still knew the way, even in the dark. But then it had often been dark when she came here. Fifteen years old, half-child, half-not-yet-woman and with the pain of her mother's death still fresh inside her, slipping out of her bedroom window into the ladder-like branches of her friendly apple tree and from there into the freedom of the night. Barefoot, too, like now. No wonder her feet knew the way.

The hill was steeper now, with roots and brambles to catch at her in the darkness. Amber found herself stumbling, the close fit of her taffeta dress catching her knees as she climbed. She tripped, dropping her shoes, then caught herself. But not before she heard the stitches rip.

'You clumsy child... Why can't you keep your clothes nice?' Aunt Bella's voice seemed to come floating back to her over the years and Amber felt herself flush with the same awkward shame that her aunt's criticism had always induced. But there was rebellion there too; there always had been, under the surface. Only somehow she had lost touch with it over the years.

On a sudden impulse, she stopped, and, hardly realising what she was doing, reached back for the zip, slipping it down so that the dress fell open at the back. The cool air caressed her skin through the thin silk slip—a pre-wedding gift from Simon—that she wore beneath.

One movement shrugged the dress from her shoulders and it fell stiffly round her feet. She picked it up and went on, revelling in the freedom and the closeness to nature she had felt all those years ago, wandering the woods in her summer nightgown. It had seemed only natural then, as it did now.

Amber shook her head and felt the pins that held her heavy auburn curls in place fall free. Normally she hated her hair loose, preferring to keep its flyaway strands and vivid colouring under tight control. Only the knowledge that, short, it would have resembled an orange dandelion clock after the first puff of wind kept her from having the whole mass shorn. But now, it was as if the years between had melted away. Leaving her in her innocence.

And then she came on it; her thinking-place. That too was just the same: hidden until you were almost upon it and then the sudden opening up of the trees to the sky and the green carpet of moss and leaves beneath the feet. The pool of faint moonlight and the feeling of moisture. Everything was just the same.

Including the fact that she was not alone.

He was standing at the far side of the clearing, next to the big oak, her special tree. In the moonlight, he looked as massive in his way as the oak's trunk; rooted in the earth. Amber looked at him without surprise, only with a growing sense of recognition. It was as if she had been expecting him.

He had been here before, that last time. How could she have forgotten? Only now his black hair was shorter and there were lines of pain etched on his forehead... And something she didn't understand was burning behind his dark eyes.

'Uncle Jake.'

'Well, if it isn't the blushing bride.' That wasn't right. His voice was harsh; angry, not warm like she remembered. 'And I'm not your damned uncle. I'm just the cuckoo in the nest, remember? We're not even related. So what the hell are you doing here, Amber?'

She felt her eyes fill with tears. 'I came to think.' The words seemed to come from a long way away. From years away... 'This is my thinking-place,' she tried again. 'I always come here.'

'Always, Amber?' Whether it was he or she who had moved, she wasn't quite sure. But they were quite close now and the words no more than a whisper. But still she could sense his anger. 'When was the last time?'

'The night you kissed me.' Where the words came from, she didn't know, except that she knew they were true.

'So you do remember,' he breathed. And again there was that something in his eyes that she didn't understand. A mixture of anger and—and what? A kind of hunger...

But she did remember. Where had it hidden, that memory, these past seven years? Somewhere in the dark recesses of her mind, like a summer flower pressed and forgotten between the pages of a book. Only then one day you opened the book again, and the flower fell out. And for a moment you were transported back as the papery petals glowed in your hand, unfaded by years and still with the ghostly scent of summer perfume.

It all seemed so long ago now. It had been a strange summer, full of upsets and tensions. Looking back, it seemed to mark the end of her childhood.

At fifteen, nearly sixteen, Amber had wanted everything to go on being the same, but, around her, her friends were changing. Sandra, two years older, had left school and was going away to secretarial college in the autumn—paid for, with unusual generosity, by her mother's employer. And Simon had seemed more interested in sitting around on the grass and talking to Sandra than in playing the exciting games that had been a feature of earlier summers. Games like Tigers in the Woods ...

And 'Uncle' Jake ... Yes, Jake had been there too, remote and awe-inspiring from the height of his twenty-four years, which was why she'd called him 'uncle'. For a while, he had deigned to amuse his little red-haired cousin. And she had worshipped him, following him around with the intense devotion of childhood. And something more. Something that Amber hadn't understood, but that had made her skin burn strangely at every accidental touch ...

For a while, she had been in heaven. But then, quite suddenly, Jake had changed. He had drawn back, cold and distant, and after that she had hardly seen him. Until that night ...

He had been here, that last night, and they had talked for hours about things she hardly understood. And then he had kissed her ... And that kiss had made a lot of things quite clear. About growing up. About being a woman——

Only now, nothing was clear. And reality and memory were shimmering, mingling, together. She didn't, couldn't speak. As if she was waiting.

'Amber.' He spoke just the one word, but it was enough to roll back the years. And then the warmth of his mouth on hers was no longer a memory and the closeness of him and the hard strength of his body against her was more real than anything she had ever felt... As his lips consumed her, Amber felt her legs buckle gently beneath her. And the moss was cool and damp against her back.

His face was above her, silhouetted against the starry blackness of the sky, the trees rising on all sides around them, like sentinels. His fingers tangled in her hair, digging into the peaty softness of the earth beneath. Pinning her down. 'You're not a child now, Amber,' she heard him say softly. 'You're a woman. And I'm a man.'

His words awakened something deep inside her: a hunger she had always known but never recognised; a void that yearned to be filled. As if in a dream she felt his hands slide over her braless breasts, their nakedness clearly visible through the transparent silk.

Simon's gift... For a moment the mists cleared and she struggled to sit up, gasping for breath as if she were drowning. But then, unbelievably, Jake's mouth closed on her breast, his tongue teasing the wet silk against her skin with such artistry that her body arched towards him, racked with a pleasure that was nearly pain.

And she was lost in the dream. As if from a great distance, she heard her own voice cry out, wordlessly, wantonly. And they were swept forward, a torrent of desire carrying them like leaves in a flood. Towards an ecstasy that she had never known or guessed existed. Towards a conflagration that consumed her body and soul. Towards a sleep as pure and dreamless as the dew on the moss.

And towards the horror of waking. And knowing what she had done.

It was cold when she woke. Damp and cold. And her body felt strangely different, as if it no longer belonged to her and might refuse to obey her commands.

Where was she? And what had happened to the blankets? For a few moments, Amber let herself hover uncertainly between sleep and waking, drugged by the languorous sensation of fulfilment that still lulled her body, searching half-heartedly for memories which instinct told her she didn't want to find.

Something lay heavily across her waist, holding her down, and Amber shifted to dislodge it. But it didn't move; or at least, not in the way she had expected. Instead, her eyes jerked open and she had to stifle a scream. Jake Farrell's brown hand was caressing her naked stomach. And, as she watched in horror, it started to climb inexorably upwards. Towards her equally naked breasts.

The memories flooded back. Amber twisted herself free, her headache for the moment forgotten, then held her breath in horror as she waited for him to wake. But all that happened was that Jake moved sleepily, and murmured something that might have been her name.

She watched in agony as his hand felt around for the warmth it had lost. But at last his fingers tangled in the crumpled silk of her discarded slip and his breathing lengthened into the steady rhythm of sleep.

Amber's only thought was to get away, as if by running she could turn back the clock. Her dress lay, earth-stained and abandoned, a few feet from where they had lain—together. But she mustn't think about that. Her hands shook with haste as she tugged the stiff silk taffeta down over her head; over her naked breasts, where his mouth——

No! Reaching awkwardly behind her she pulled up the zip with a violence that caught a strand of red-gold hair and almost ripped it from her scalp, making her gasp with the pain and then freeze with terror again in case she had wakened him. But still he slept.

Her shoes... She looked around helplessly, then remembered dropping them when she fell. She would never find them again in the grey half-darkness. Well, she would have to do without. And the same went for the slip that his hand was still clutching. There was no way she could risk waking the sleeping man at her feet in an effort to regain that wisp of silk. Somehow, not waking him seemed of vital importance. If only she could escape unseen, she felt illogically, then she would be safe.

And yet, now it came to it, Amber found it strangely difficult to leave the glade, as if a part of her was still held by its enchantment. As if it were really her lover she was leaving, instead of a stranger...

Amber looked down at the man whose body she had known so intimately and yet whom she didn't really know at all. Her eyes were used to the darkness now, and she could see his hard,

muscled limbs sprawled with magnificent care-
lessness on the soft green moss, his arm still
crooked where he had held her close in their sleep.
There was nothing apologetic about his nakedness, she thought. He lay like some pagan god
of the forest, utterly at home.

And utterly male. Amber felt her stomach
clench with desire and turned hurriedly away, her
face hot with shame. How could she think like
that when her marriage to Simon was only a day
away? And how could she have——? But she
wasn't ready to think of that yet. Deliberately
making her mind a blank, she started to pick her
way down carefully through the trees.

By the time she reached the outskirts of the
village, it was almost dawn. Her mind seemed as
cold and stiff as her body, the lightness of spirit
with which she had entered the wood as far away
as a dream.

And yet—there *was* an unaccustomed
lightness... For a moment, the sensation eluded
her. Then, with mounting horror, she looked
down at her hands.

What she saw there drained the blood from
her face.

The ring was gone.

CHAPTER TWO

'YOUR engagement ring? Oh, Amber, no! Where did you lose it—in the woods? Why on earth didn't you go back and look for it?'

Slumped over Sandra's kitchen table, staring wearily at the telltale gap on the third finger of her left hand, Amber dredged her tired brain for an explanation that wasn't too far from the truth. 'I couldn't go back,' she said at last, honestly enough. 'I didn't realise it was gone until I was almost here, and by then... I was so tired, Sandra. I just couldn't face going back.'

'Tired! You were practically delirious—muttering about enchanted glades and pagan gods and goodness knows what else.' She hesitated a moment and then ploughed on. 'Amber, you have to tell me what happened last night. Someone obviously attacked you. I think we should call the police.'

Amber took a sip of her third cup of strong coffee, before opening her mouth to protest. But her friend still ploughed determinedly on. 'Look, I should have done it last night when you arrived, but I didn't dare risk upsetting you any more. You were so peculiar... For a while there, I wondered if someone had slipped some sort of drug into your drink at that nightclub.'

'No one slipped anything into my drink— except alcohol. I was drunk, Sandra, that was all.' Amber felt her cheeks redden at the deliberate untruth. 'I had too much to drink and I stupidly decided to walk it off in the woods. And then I got lost and fell down a bank and got myself into a bit of a mess. And that's all.'

If she said if often enough, she thought, she might even convince herself. Although somehow she knew that, even if she persuaded her mind to forget what had really happened, her body would never lose the memory of his touch... Even after two baths and a complete change of clothes, she still felt as if the marks of Jake's lovemaking were emblazoned on her flesh.

Like a brand of shame. But the worst of it was that beneath the shame lurked the memory of ecstasy, and part of her ached for the pleasure that he had given her. A part of her that she must have inherited from her mother, that had lain unsuspected until Jake Farrell awakened it. A part of her that wasn't concerned with morals, or decency, but with passion and desire...

'I don't believe you. You weren't drunk, Amber—I was watching you, and you drank less than I did. And I didn't go wandering around in the dark and falling down banks and losing valuable rings.'

Her friend's tone of sarcasm made it apparent that she wasn't convinced. Amber sighed, knowing how stubborn Sandra could be when she got the bit between her teeth.

'You were out there for three hours, for goodness' sake—those woods aren't big enough to get lost in for more than ten minutes. And don't tell me you were thinking. That's what you told me last night, and it just doesn't wash. I know lots of people who think and they don't appear on my doorstep at three o'clock in the morning looking as if they've just gone three rounds with King Kong.'

'I told you, I fell——'

'Down a bank—yes, I know. And presumably that's where you lost your ring? Not to mention your shoes and your underwear?'

Amber felt the colour drain from her face, and Sandra's voice filled with sympathy.

'I helped you undress, remember?' she said gently. 'Amber, poor darling, I know how you must feel. And I realise you're afraid it will spoil your wedding and you're probably scared stiff of what Simon's reaction will be. But you must see you can't just pretend it didn't happen. Simon's bound to notice that you've lost his ring, and, beside that, you need looking after. You may——' She swallowed and looked down, avoiding Amber's eyes. 'You may need medical treatment. For goodness' sake, Amber, if he—if this man raped you, you might even be pregnant.'

'No! No, it wasn't—he didn't rape me.'

This time, though she knew Sandra would misinterpret her words, they nevertheless carried the ring of truth. The other girl relaxed visibly. 'Thank goodness for that! But there was a man, then? And something did happen?'

'Yes...' The word dragged out reluctantly. 'Yes, something did happen. But I'm not hurt, and I just want to forget about it.'

'But Amber, you can't! If there's some man going around attacking women, you have to report it! What happens if next time——?'

'There won't be a next time, Sandra.' Amber felt as if she were picking her way across a bog, trying to step from one small safe fact to another across the giant morass of the truth. 'It wasn't— he wasn't a stranger. It was—someone I used to know. He was angry about my marrying Simon, that's all.'

Well, that was true enough. Although why Jake Farrell should have cared one way or the other about her marriage she wasn't quite sure. But she had felt the anger in him, like a cold flame.

She shivered. 'But it wasn't... He wouldn't have forced me.'

And that was the truth too, the savage truth that tore at her heart. He hadn't needed to force her. She had been only too willing... 'Oh, please, Sandra? How would you like to spend the start of your married life in a police station?'

She could sense the other girl weakening and pressed home the point. 'Promise me, please. Simon will be coming to pick me up any moment now, and I don't want him to find out...'

But as soon as the words were out of her mouth Amber realised it was the wrong argument to have used. She thought of Sandra so much as 'her' friend that she was inclined to forget that before Simon and herself had become romantically involved the three of them had been equally close. In fact, as a native of Marchings, Sandra had known Simon even longer than she had herself. And where his interests were threatened, as

Amber had discovered before, she couldn't always rely on the other girl's unquestioning support.

Her heart sank as Sandra's face stiffened with a new determination. 'You mean you're not even going to tell him? Amber, you must! How can you possibly start off your married life by keeping a secret like that? And anyway, he's bound to notice about the ring. So how are you going to explain that away?'

Amber leapt in eagerly. 'That's what I was going to ask you—could you go and look for it? I know just where it will be. I'd go myself, but my aunt's arranged a big family lunch today, and I really can't miss it. Then I could tell Simon that it came off last night and I'd given it to you for safe-keeping . . .'

But her voice petered out in the face of the other girl's frigid disapproval. 'I'm sorry, Amber, but I won't help you lie to Simon.' Sandra sounded uncomfortable, but resolutely firm. 'Quite apart from the fact that you need his support, I think he has a right to know. He's going to be your husband, for goodness' sake! If he loves you, it won't make any difference. You ought to trust him.'

If only it were that straightforward . . . Amber felt a deep sense of shame at her own inability to match Sandra's sturdy honesty. 'Oh, Sandra— I do. But don't you see? If I told him now, he'd want to rush off and *do* something, but there wouldn't be anything he could do. It would only upset him, and spoil the wedding.' The argument sounded weak, even to herself. 'And then Aunt

Bella will find out—and she'll never believe that it wasn't somehow my fault.'

That was better; she could see the sympathy returning to her friend's face. Amber felt another pang of disgust at herself for being so manipulative as she pressed the argument home. 'You know she secretly thinks I'm some kind of scarlet woman, just because of the way my mother behaved after she left my father,' she reminded the other girl. 'If it weren't for the fact that I'm undeniably "Family", I doubt if she'd ever have agreed to our engagement. But this could stir it all up again. It would ruin our wedding-day.'

She hated herself for doing it, but she was getting through... Ever since she had come to live permanently in the village after her mother's death, Sandra had been her refuge against her aunt's censorious discipline.

For a lonely moment, Amber wished she could tell her friend the truth. But she knew it was impossible. How could she admit that on the eve of her wedding she had let herself be seduced by a ghost from the past? That she had lost her virginity to a man she hardly knew? Or that she had welcomed his wild, animal lovemaking like some sort of wild thing herself?

Hot with shame, Amber watched the emotions battling it out on Sandra's face and sighed with relief as at last the other girl nodded. 'Well, all right, then. I'll keep quiet—for Simon's sake as much as yours. And I'll look for the ring and bring it round tomorrow. But you have to promise you'll tell him after the wedding.'

'Of course.' But, even as she made the promise, Amber knew she had no intention of keeping it. She couldn't afford the luxury of confession. In the sleepless hours since she had arrived barefoot and hysterical at her friend's door, she had come to two very definite conclusions.

The first was that she would go ahead with the wedding. Of that she was certain: all the doubts and hesitations of the past few days had vanished completely with her new-found clarity of vision. She would marry Simon and she would spend the rest of her life repaying a debt that he would never know she owed...

Because that was the other decision. She would say nothing, ever, to anyone about what had happened. That would be her penance; she would have to bear it alone. But she owed it to Simon to make certain that he would never hear about it from another source; never suffer the shame of knowing his bride had betrayed him.

So no one would ever know. Except for herself, of course—and Jake. But she would do everything she could to blot the episode from her consciousness, and as for Jake—well, it wasn't the kind of story he'd want to get around. What man would boast of seducing his cousin's bride-to-be?

No, Jake would hardly say anything.

Would he?

Of course Jake wouldn't say anything. Amber bit her lip and tried to concentrate on what Simon was saying.

'You left your ring round at Sandra's? Well, really, Amber—I do think you could have taken more care.' He sounded aggrieved and rather pompous. 'I don't know what my mother will say. It is a very valuable piece, after all. The Family will be expecting to see it. And you will need it for the ceremony tomorrow...' He stopped and frowned at his watch. 'Perhaps we should go back now and fetch it.'

'Oh, no, Simon, not now. There isn't time.' Amber's sleepless night was beginning to avenge itself in the shape of a headache which throbbed unmercifully behind her eyes, and she was beginning to wish she hadn't promised to be back for family lunch. With sick certainty, she knew that she wasn't going to be able to eat a thing. But at least it provided her with an excuse. And Mrs Farrell's strict regard for time-keeping made it a valid one.

'Perhaps you're right; it wouldn't do to be late. Oh, and did I tell you? As an extra present, Mother has decided to have our part of the house redecorated throughout while we're in Bali. It really is very generous of her, and naturally she has so much more experience in these matters——'

Amber smiled wanly, feeling like an actress playing a part in a rather bad play. It seemed all wrong to be walking along the street with Simon like this, talking about wedding presents. As if everything were normal... But then, as far as he was concerned, everything *was* normal. And it was up to her to make sure that was how it stayed.

'That's very kind of her,' she managed. The last thing she wanted was to come back from honeymoon to find Mrs Farrell's taste in wallpaper all over her walls, but at that moment she simply couldn't find the energy to protest. The honeymoon itself seemed such a barrier that she could hardly believe that there might come a day when it would be in the past, and things like wallpaper would actually matter...

'I'm sorry, Simon,' she murmured. 'I don't exactly feel... I had rather a lot to drink last night.' She realised guiltily that she was wandering further and further from the truth, but it was the obvious excuse. 'It might be better if I skipped lunch.'

'Nonsense. All the more reason for having something to eat. I was out last night as well, remember, but I had a proper breakfast and I feel fine.' He put his arm round her shoulder as they turned into the long drive up to the Hall. 'Besides, all The Family are here—even the uncles.'

'The uncles' were Aunt Bella's unmarried brothers, and Amber tried to suppress her surge of irritation at the way Simon followed his mother's lead in treating the four confirmed bachelors so disparagingly. She had always found them rather restful... But, like Grandfather Matthew, whose overwhelming personality Amber still remembered vividly, Aunt Bella had little use for those who chose not to further The Family. And now she noticed that Simon had started to capitalise the word in just the same way.

Amber found herself flinching away from his touch, and wondered for the first time if she was really capable of carrying through her deception. If only there was more time; time to forget. Time for her body to forget . . . What chance would she have on her wedding night, if she jumped at a casual contact? The excuse of bridal nerves could only be carried so far . . .

But what could she do? Delay the wedding? She could imagine the amused disbelief which would meet that suggestion.

'But, my dear Amber,' her aunt would say, looking down at her as if she was suggesting that the world should be moved on its axis, 'we've ordered the *marquee*.' And that would be that; just as it always was when Mrs Farrell pronounced.

Simon's father came to the door to greet them, and Amber gave him a hug. She liked her uncle and father-in-law-to-be almost as much as she disliked the sharp-nosed woman he had married, and whose family name he had meekly agreed to take. And she admired him for the quiet and yet determined way he stood up to his overbearing wife. She suspected that without his support there would have been a lot more opposition to the idea of her marriage to Simon.

In fact, it had amazed her how readily her aunt had consented. One minute, it had seemed, Amber was being hustled straight from boarding school to the university course that she strongly suspected was just an excuse for getting her out of the way. And the next, Simon had been meeting her at the station at the end of her first term, telling her that he thought it was time they got engaged . . .

'Hello, gorgeous.' Her uncle kissed her warmly and ushered them in through the imposing doorway. 'Did you have a good time last night? I'm afraid it's a bit of a crush here. The Farrells are out in force. In fact, guess who's turned up?'

'Hello, Uncle Bob.' Amber followed him into the house, a twinge of genuine curiosity over-laying her worries. 'I've no idea.' Perhaps it would be all right after all. Perhaps by tomorrow it would all seem like a bad dream...

'Da *daaa*!' As they entered the room, Mr Farrell flung his hand out in a sweeping gesture towards a tall figure standing by the window with his back to the room. 'Look who's here!'

Amber looked. The figure turned round and moved away from the light, walking towards her into the room. It was Jake Farrell. And, with his broad shoulders silhouetted against the brightness of the window, he looked far too substantial to be the figment of anyone's dream.

Unthinkingly, Amber stepped forward. Their eyes met, and time seemed to slow down and stop, locking them into a private world, trapped like flies in the amber that had given her her name.

With part of her mind, Amber was aware of Simon's voice, somewhere behind her. But it meant less than nothing. The world was a pair of deep-set, dark eyes and a mouth twisted with anger. Or was it pain? And in that long moment she knew she was his entirely. He could have stepped forward; taken her; claimed her. And she would have done nothing to resist.

But the moment passed, and, slowly, the world began to spin again. Amber tore her eyes away. And the babble of sound became words and re-claimed her attention.

'The prodigal returns,' said Simon's father with dry humour. He seemed cheerfully unaware of any untoward effects of his 'surprise', Amber noted with relief, her mind already recovering from its temporary paralysis. 'There he was, looking as if he'd spent the night in a haystack, and announcing that he'd come for the wedding.'

'It was my car.' It was a shock to hear him speak, and his voice was deeper than she remembered. But then, last night, they had hardly spoken above a whisper. Had hardly needed to speak at all. 'A Porsche, not a haystack—quite comfortable, if a bit cramped. I didn't want to disturb you last night. I arrived—rather later than I planned.'

All the time he was speaking, Amber could feel his eyes on her, as if he was speaking to her uncle with only the surface of his words. As if he was waiting for something from her—for what, she wasn't sure.

'You should have woken us, Jacob. We would have been delighted to see you.' Mrs Farrell came forward, carrying glasses of pale sherry which she distributed among her guests with studied graciousness. But Amber was certain that beneath her impeccable manner her aunt was far from pleased. In fact, she radiated hostility...

For a few moments, Amber's imagination went into overdrive. What if her aunt had found out? What if Jake had told her? But a more rational train of thought reassured her that, if that had been so, Aunt Bella would hardly have been making even the most brittle of polite conversation with her niece's seducer. She had always

disapproved of Jake, that Amber remembered.
Because of his not really being Family... His
father had been adopted.

Yes, that was right. A son of some partner
who'd died. Jake's words from the night before
came back to her. 'A cuckoo in the nest,' he had
called himself. But she suppressed the thought
quickly. Now, of all times, she couldn't afford
to remember...

At that moment, her aunt handed her a sherry
and Amber reached out for it unthinkingly. There
was a sharp intake of breath.

'Amber! Where is your ring? Why are you not
wearing it?'

'Oh—it came off last night, Auntie, and I gave
it to Sandra to look after...' She could feel Jake's
eyes on her as she laboured through the increas-
ingly feeble-sounding explanation she had prepared. Did he guess she was lying? Had he
noticed last night that she was wearing it?
Somehow, she was certain that he knew—and
that he was enjoying her discomfiture. Under his
mocking gaze, she could feel the back of her neck
prickle hot with shame and fear. If he spoke...

But for the time being, at least, he was silent.
And before her aunt could produce more than a,
'Well, really, Amber...' her uncle had swept in
to propose a toast of welcome to the newcomer.

Somehow, Amber managed to join in the
general murmur as the others raised their glasses.
'Welcome home, Jake.' Her voice was a mere
whisper in the chorus. So why did she feel that
it was to her and her alone that he replied?

'I had to come back,' he said seriously. 'To see——' He broke off, but his eyes never left her face. 'I'd been away too long.'

'You have, Jake.' Simon's father nodded with cheery amiability. 'If you'd let Simon know before that you were coming back for the wedding, you could have been his best man. As it is, he's asked a friend of his to do it. Though I suppose——'

'No!' For the first time, Amber felt Jake's attention shift from her as he explosively rejected the half-formed suggestion. 'No, you mustn't think of it,' he added more calmly, though she could still detect an unusual level of agitation in his voice. 'It wouldn't be fair on Simon's friend. And besides——'

Like the sun emerging from a cloudbank, the heat of his gaze swept over her again, drying her mouth with apprehension—though of what, she wasn't sure. But she could feel something hanging by the thinnest of threads over her head. 'Besides what?' she tried to say casually, but it came out as a meaningless croak.

With her usual disregard for other people's conversations, Mrs Farrell chose that moment to start shepherding her guests in the direction of the dining-room. Amber thought for a moment that the subject had been dropped, but as they trooped out into the passageway she found herself trapped between Jake's rangy body and Simon's stockier, more yielding frame.

She held her breath, trying desperately not to let their bodies touch. But to her horror she felt Jake's hand reach out to stroke her tightly knotted hair, running a stray strand of red-gold through his fingers. And heard him say, 'After all, Simon, I might be tempted to steal the bride away from you. Little Amber has changed a lot since we used to play Tigers in the Woods.'

His tone was superficially light-hearted and Amber prayed that she was the only one to hear the meaning behind his words—and prayed also that he would be content with making barbed comments that only she could understand. It was plain enough now that he intended to make her suffer for what had happened between them the previous night.

Probably he was angry on Simon's behalf as well as his own—as a sort of honorary elder brother, it would be reasonable enough, although the two of them had never been close. And his own feelings of guilt would fuel his anger. If only she could be sure that he would stop at punishing *her*... If only she could be certain that he wouldn't tell.

But she couldn't be sure, Amber realised, as she picked at the food that was placed in front of her, eating nothing and hardly noticing the comments about 'pre-wedding jitters' that her lack of appetite prompted. The old Jake would never have betrayed her, but, seeing him here, she could sense a difference in him. This man was a stranger, an unknown quantity. And the only way to know she was safe would be to ask him.

'Jake and I will make the coffee,' Amber announced in a carefully casual voice when that interminable meal was finally ended. 'I'm sure Mrs Atkins has plenty to do getting ready for—for tomorrow.' She couldn't quite bring herself to say 'for the wedding'. 'And this is the last chance I'll have to catch up on Jake's news. I've got a million things to see to.'

She half expected—half hoped?—that he might object, but, if it was a hope, it was in vain. Jake followed her down to the kitchen, his closeness raising the hairs on the back of her neck as she made her way down the steep, old-fashioned stairs. As he followed her through the door, he closed it behind them. They were alone. And his silence pressed in on her, waiting; more disconcerting than any words could have been.

It seemed an aeon before she gathered the courage to break that black silence. 'I thought— we needed to talk, Jake. About what happened.'

She paused, trying to gauge his reaction, but still he said nothing, and at last she carried on desperately, 'I—you don't have to worry about it, Jake. It—nothing like that will ever happen again, I promise. I don't know what came over me—over us. I just want to forget it ever happened.'

'Forget it?' To hear him speak was a relief; she had begun to think that his silence was just another barbed weapon to torment her. But there was a roughness in his voice like jagged steel. 'What a very convenient memory you must have, Amber. Or else you were more drunk than I realised. Are you really telling me that you could forget about last night? About the way we made love? I remember it in vivid detail, I can assure you. Including the part where you——'

'Stop it!' Amber backed away from the door in an agony of apprehension. What if someone overheard...? 'Jake, please. I realise it was my fault it happened; I'm not blaming you. But I just want to put it behind me. I'm marrying Simon in the morning, and——'

'You're what?' She started back from the explosion of angry sound that assaulted her ear. 'My God, what kind of woman are you, Amber? I know it's not exactly fashionable to be a virgin bride any more, but I believe it's still customary to start off with at least a semblance of fidelity. What does my oh, so respectable little cousin think of his bride arriving at the church all hot and steaming from another man's bed? Or is he so besotted with you that he doesn't care?'

'He doesn't know.' The angrier Jake became, the more Amber felt her own voice fade away. 'I haven't told him, Jake, and I never will. I'll make it up to him...'

'You don't love him.' The brutal words were dipped in the acid of contempt. 'How do you propose to make that up to him?'

'What happened last night was nothing to do with love.' Her voice was stronger now, and her certainty was returning. 'I am fond of him, Jake, and I——'

'And every time he takes you to bed you'll remember how it was last night. With me, Amber.'

'No!'

'Yes.' His voice was implacable, tearing at her defences. Destroying her. 'You know I'm right.

You say you don't know what came over you last night—well, I could think of several names for it, not all of them pretty. But one thing I'm damn sure of: if you loved Simon, you wouldn't have felt that way about me.'

'I'd had too much to drink, Jake. I wasn't responsible——' But even as she said it, she knew that she couldn't hide behind a lie. 'At least——'

But he broke in, angrily. 'So that's your story, is it? Only we both know it isn't true. We were both intoxicated last night, but not by alcohol. And besides——' his voice softened a little as he took her by the shoulders and shook her gently '—that's not the way it works, Tiger-eyes. Alcohol just strips away the layer of civilisation in us. It doesn't change what's underneath—it lets it out. No matter how drunk you were, if you cared enough about Simon to marry him, you'd never have responded that way to me.'

'I didn't . . .' Her voice trailed away as she saw his eyes flash with anger, realising the futility of denial.

'Didn't what, Amber? Didn't respond?' His grip on her shoulders tightened, drawing her closer, and she could feel the anger seething inside him, ready to boil. 'Are you claiming I raped you?'

'No, Jake.' Close to panic, Amber tried to push him away, desperately seeking a way to defuse the situation. But all that happened was that her fingers slipped on the coarse cotton of his shirt, flexing involuntarily as they encountered the warmth of the flesh beneath. And then his arms

were around her, crushing her arms helplessly
between their bodies. And she felt her nipples
stiffen against the backs of her hands.

He was looking down at her, cruelly tri-
umphant. Except for the pain which still showed
in his eyes. 'It's too late for regrets now, Amber.
Too late to learn to think of England and settle
for married respectability with my tedious little
cousin.'

Slowly and deliberately, he bent his mouth to
hers, and this time there was no gentleness in his
kiss, but only a savage hunger and an anger that
was close to hatred—and yet a million miles away.

Amber felt herself sinking, even as she tried to
resist the tide of desire that claimed her. But there
was no hiding the response that melted her body
into his arms and set her eyes aflame with orange
fire. And at last she abandoned even the pretence.

When he loosed her, she staggered and nearly
fell. And his words burned into her brain.

'You want me, Amber. Or are you telling me
he makes you feel like that?'

She shook her head helplessly. How could she
ever expect him to understand? 'No... He
doesn't.' And she suddenly felt a wave of longing
for the fiery passion on which she had turned her
back forever. 'But Jake—that isn't what's important. Not to me.'

She could feel his contempt burning her and
struggled to find the words with which to explain. 'I don't want that kind of relationship,
Jake. I don't want to burn up with passion for
a few months and then wake up and wonder what
I'm going to do with the rest of my life. My

mother spent her whole life running after that sort of passion, and in the end she died of it. I'm not like her—I won't be. Simon and I have known each other for a long time. We practically grew up together. And we both want the same things——'

'Do you? Are you sure, Amber?' His voice was almost hypnotically compelling. 'I don't think you are. You want to be, but you're your mother's daughter.'

'No...' But all fight, all will, seemed gone.

'You can't be sure.' He stretched out his hand to where her hair gleamed red-gold beneath the light from the kitchen window, and drew her roughly back towards him.

'You can't be sure that you can live without this...'

CHAPTER THREE

OF COURSE Jake wouldn't say anything. He had tried to persuade her, and he had failed. She had made it clear that she wasn't prepared to jeopardise her relationship with Simon for the sake of a purely physical attraction, and now he would leave her alone.

At least she hoped she had made it clear... Somehow, she had found the strength to push him away and had run back to the sanctuary of the dining-room. And he had followed with the fast-cooling coffee and said nothing untoward. Surely, if he had meant to betray her, he would have spoken then.

Surely... Amber bit her lip and tried to turn her concentration back to the problem of packing for a honeymoon in Bali. Ironically for one of Matthew Farrell's descendants, the most exotic holiday she had had since her mother's death were a few weeks in the South of France with a girl she had met at university. A childhood spent almost constantly on the move with her mother had given her a strong taste for staying at home.

What should she take? Amber tried to conjure up a picture of what a honeymoon with Simon would consist of, but failed miserably. Would he expect her to dress for dinner? The brochure said 'casual', but he had given her two new evening dresses, so presumably he would expect her to wear them. And then there was the 'surprise' hotel he had insisted on organising for the two nights before their departure. She had no idea what that would be like; but, if she knew Simon, it was likely to be stuffily formal and very luxurious.

The suitcase stared up at her, still almost empty. They had almost lived out of suitcases in the old days—at least that was what it had seemed like to Amber. No sooner had she been settled with one set of long-suffering friends or relations than Claudine would swoop in and carry her off to her latest establishment. And then it would all break up, among dramatic recriminations, and the cycle would begin again with her mother's latest lover.

Only just now, Amber realised, she didn't want to think about her mother. She had an uncomfortable feeling that the lovely, talented and completely irresponsible Claudine Ashley would have dismissed Simon with a barely concealed yawn as 'Too, too boring, darling'. And that what had happened with Jake the night before had been much more her mother's kind of *affaire*.

'There was no passion left, my darling,' she had explained to her little daughter when Amber had asked why they weren't going to live with Daddy any more. 'One must have passion...' Then, realising perhaps that it wasn't an ideal explanation for a confused nine-year-old, she had kissed her and swept her into her arms and added that comforting panacea, 'You'll understand when you're older, darling.' And Amber had filed it away for the day when it would all become clear.

Only, before that could happen, Claudine had died of what Amber later realised had probably been a semi-deliberate overdose after the break-up of her latest relationship. And Amber had come to live at the Hall.

There, she had gradually come to realise just how lacking in stability her upbringing had been, following her mother as she flitted from one 'passion' to another. And, although she had never been able to give her rather severe and for-bidding aunt the adoration she had given her butterfly mother, she was grateful for the solid foundation Mrs Farrell had given her life.

Well, now she too had experienced passion, if that was what it was. Only, unlike her mother, she had no intention of letting such an irrespon-sible emotion rule her life. Just for a moment, Amber let her thoughts go back to the tumult of sensations that had thrown her helplessly into Jake Farrell's arms, but even in memory they overwhelmed her. She shivered and dragged her mind away.

How could she have allowed herself to behave so—wantonly? Although perhaps it was a blessing in disguise. It had effectively cleared away the doubts that had shadowed her engage-ment to Simon. She had been worried that her feelings for her fiancé had been too cool; but now she knew that passion was nothing to do with caring——

'Amber, dear, telephone for you.'

Her aunt's unusually friendly voice floated up the stairs, jolting her out of her reverie. 'Just coming, Aunt Bella.' With sudden resolution she folded the two evening dresses and placed them neatly in the case. Simon had bought them, after all, along with the rest of her trousseau. No doubt he knew best what was suitable.

And if she needed more, she planned as she hurried downstairs, she would just let Simon kit her out when they reached their destination. She could imagine the proprietorial pleasure he would take in accompanying her to the shops. 'I want to buy a dress for my wife...'

'Amber.'

The voice on the phone hit her like a winding blow, leaving her speechless, her mind in a panicky spin. Only when she heard her name repeated impatiently did she manage to croak a response.

'Amber—are you there? We have to talk.'

'I—I'm here, Jake. But I don't think we have anything to say.' She cast a worried look behind her, but to her relief her aunt had disappeared back to her preoccupation with lists and arrangements. 'I told you—you don't have to worry about me, Jake. I know what I'm doing.'

'Do you? I don't think you do.' There was a long pause, and Amber knew she ought just to replace the receiver. But as if he had guessed her intention Jake spoke again.

'Amber, just listen, will you? Don't hang up.' His voice was almost reasonable now, not savage as it had been before. 'Just let me have my say and then I'll leave you alone.'

He was waiting for her to answer. She ought to finish it now. But a voice that she hardly knew as her own whispered, 'Yes?'

'Good girl. Now, listen to me, Amber. This business has knocked you backwards, and no wonder. It's taken me by surprise as well, and that's why I haven't been dealing with it rationally. I frightened you earlier; I've made it worse. And I'm sorry. But there isn't much time. So forget about me, Tiger-eyes. Whether you want to see me again is neither here nor there. That can wait. But whatever happens, you can't marry Simon. Both of us know you don't love him——'

She tried to interrupt, but his voice, deep and urgent, rode over her objections. 'Just listen, Amber. You don't love Simon; you even admitted as much. Right now, you don't think that matters. You think that's what you want. But I've tried that sort of marriage, and I know the hell it can turn into. I don't know how much you know about me, Amber; how much Simon has said about me——'

'Nothing.' Her voice was stronger now. 'Why should he? I thought you'd gone away...'

Jake gave a short laugh, but there was no amusement in it. 'Well, I'm back now. Look, Amber, there isn't time to go into details about my history. All you have to know is that I married...soon after I last saw you. For what seemed like adequate reasons at the time. And I damn near wrecked three lives by doing it.'

There was a gruffness in his tone that spoke of real emotion, and Amber felt herself respond. Perhaps he did care...

'And I can't bear to see the same happen to you, Tiger-eyes,' he pressed on. 'You don't have to make any final decisions now. All I'm asking you to do is wait. To delay the wedding and think things out...'

'I can't!' Amber's voice rose almost to a wail before she checked it in panic. 'My aunt——'

'Then I'll help you. You don't have to do anything, Amber. Just be in the glade tonight.'

He must have heard the hiss of her breath. 'You can slip out again; you always could, I remember. I'll be there, and I'll take you away. You won't have to talk to anyone; I'll do the explaining. I'll tell them you need a breathing-space——'

'No! No, I can't.' And then, almost against her will, 'What...what time?'

'I'll be there from midnight.' She could feel the intensity of his purpose, burning down the wires. Willing her... 'And I'll wait as long as it takes.'

'Jake, I——' But, before she could say anything, the receiver had clicked back into place and there was nothing but the distant whirring of the exchange. And Amber sank down on to the hallway carpet and burst into tears.

'I knew it.' Her aunt's voice sounded grimly behind her and Amber's stomach clenched with renewed panic. How much had Aunt Bella heard? 'I thought I recognised that voice,' she went on.

'What's he been saying to you, you silly girl? Is he trying to cause trouble?'

'I don't know what you mean,' Amber said weakly, her thoughts spinning in confusion inside her head. It was almost as though her aunt knew—but that was impossible. 'Is who out to cause trouble?'

'Don't be a fool, child,' the older woman said briskly. 'That was Jacob Farrell on the phone— I blame myself for not realising from the start, or I would have dealt with him myself. Am I right?'

'Yes,' Amber whispered.

'I thought as much. And it is abundantly clear to me that he has said something to upset you. So I suggest you stop behaving in this uncontrolled fashion and listen to me while I tell you a few home truths about that young man. There are two sides to every story, Amber. And when you've heard the other side of his, you may feel less inclined to make an exhibition of yourself.'

Bewildered, Amber followed her aunt into her private sitting-room and sat down at a small table while the other woman rang for tea. What on earth was her aunt talking about? And how could she have known about Jake? Amber knew that she ought to be planning what she was going to say, but she didn't have the energy to think coherently. 'Aunt Bella——' she started hesitantly.

'We'll wait for the tea to arrive. I see no reason why Mrs Atkins should be permitted to regale the whole village with tales of your foolishness.' So they waited until the housekeeper arrived with the tray, looking curiously at Amber's tear-stained face but presenting a well-trained silence.

'I've put sugar in it. Perhaps that will help you to get a grip on yourself.' Her aunt handed her a cup and watched while Amber took a tentative sip, wrinkling her nose at the unaccustomed sweetness. 'Now, are you going to tell me what Jacob said, or shall I tell you?'

Amber said nothing. But she had the strangest feeling that she didn't want to hear what her aunt was about to tell her; that despite her comforting words it would be something that would cut her to the heart. Her aunt took her silence as consent.

'So then I'll tell you. Jacob Farrell told you about my father's will, didn't he?'

She must have misinterpreted Amber's open-mouthed look of amazement because she sailed on. 'I see that I'm right. And no doubt he managed to impugn my son's motives in wishing to marry you?'

'He——' Amber's voice seemed to stick in her throat and her aunt looked at her with something close to dislike.

'You needn't answer, since you have apparently lost the power of rational speech. And besides, I have no wish to know exactly what lies that reprehensible young man chose to tell you. I shall tell you the truth about my father's testamentary dispositions, Amber. And then you will judge for yourself.'

Coolly, she poured herself a second cup of tea and took a sip before continuing.

'As you are aware, Amber, or would be if you had ever showed the proper interest in your

family and heritage, your grandfather, Matthew,
was very much a family man. As well as his own
six children, he also adopted Jacob's father—the
son of a business partner who died.' She paused
and took another sip of tea.

'A mistake, in my view. He could have provided for the boy without going to such ex-
tremes. But that is beside the point. My father
believed strongly in the importance of The Family
and was greatly disappointed when so few of his
children took a properly responsible attitude in
these matters. As you know, with the exception
of Jacob's father, your uncles have all main-
tained their bachelor status and your
mother——'

She broke off with an expression of distaste.
'The less said about your mother's disgraceful
behaviour, the better. The result was that Jacob's
father and I were the only two of our generation
to choose to uphold The Family. And Jacob's
parents died some years ago. Leaving only
myself.'

'But what——?'

'Don't interrupt, child. My father rightly decided that, as a woman, I would hardly like to
succeed him in the business, and unfortunately
your uncle has never shown any aptitude for
commercial activity. Accordingly, when your
grandfather died four years ago, he preferred to
bequeath the ownership and control of Farrell
Travel directly to those he regarded as his two
grandsons.'

She sniffed in obvious disapproval. 'That is,
Simon and Jacob. Your grandfather had always

been rather taken in by Jacob, despite the fact that he chose to set up some foolish enterprise of his own instead of entering the business as my father had planned.'

Amber stared blankly at her aunt. 'To Simon and Jacob? But I thought... Simon told me...' She could hear Simon's rather pedantic voice telling her of his prospects, and exactly why she should not hesitate to accept his proposal. 'I thought Simon inherited everything on his marriage?'

'As things have turned out, that is in essence what will happen. But in fact the bequest was somewhat more complicated than that.' The older woman took a deep breath, and for the first time Amber realised that her aunt was not her normal confident self. She was actually nervous...

'Your grandfather's will was intended to rectify what he saw as the irresponsibility of the younger generation in the matter of marriage. Accordingly, he left control of the business to whichever of the two boys should first marry and produce a child, the business to be held in trust until those conditions were fulfilled.'

With an air of finality, she bent and replaced her cup on the tray, then crossed her hands firmly in her lap. 'Naturally,' she went on, 'this occasioned us no little anxiety. Jacob was an entirely unsuitable person to gain control of what is, after all, very much a Family business. However, my mind was to some extent set at rest by the fact that Jacob had shown absolutely no inclination up to that point to regularise his affairs. And, since my son was already... fond of you, it seemed a foregone conclusion that it would very properly be he who would inherit. I believe that this was, in fact, my father's intention, and that the will was simply his way of making his strong views on the subject known.'

She paused again and pursed her lips. But Amber was past interrupting. Her aunt was plainly about to arrive at last at the point of her narrative, and she had a cold suspicion what it was going to be.

'I had failed to account, however, for Jacob Farrell's complete lack of moral scruples. Almost immediately after probate had been granted, he contracted a marriage to a most unsuitable young woman who was apparently already carrying his child. He even had the impudence to invite me to the wedding. In a *register office* in London.'

This, to her aunt, was obviously almost as heinous a crime as the actual marriage. But Amber could scarcely take in what she was saying. She was remembering Jake's words. 'For what seemed adequate reasons at the time...' Yes, an inheritance that large must have seemed 'adequate'. But another part of her mind rebelled at condemning Jake so easily. He had sounded sincere...

'But if his girlfriend was already pregnant, Aunt Bella, couldn't it have been that he would have married her anyway? Or they might have been intending to live together; lots of people do. I know it seems unfair to Simon, but——'

Her aunt quelled her with a cold stare. 'I see he has been very persuasive. And yes, at the time I might have given him the benefit of the doubt.

Except that his wife was unfortunate enough to suffer a miscarriage almost immediately after the wedding and was warned that she should not attempt a further pregnancy for at least two years. And Jacob's response was to walk out, deserting his wife completely. She was distraught and suffered some kind of nervous breakdown, but he divorced her as soon as was legally possible. There was no question of any genuine attachment—on his side, at least.'

Amber just sat there. It was as if all the air had been knocked from her body by the blow. Her aunt smiled coldly, pleased by the effect of her words.

'So you see now why it wouldn't surprise me if he tried to make trouble between you and Simon. No doubt he has made it out to be in my son's interest to marry quickly, and to some extent that is true. But you will realise that Jacob himself has a far greater interest in preventing any such marriage. And that it would be exceedingly foolish of you to take notice of anything he says.'

'Yes. Yes, I see.' And she did see, with a cold clarity of anger that burned like a flame of ice inside her. She had thought the events of the night before had been a moment of madness on both sides; a mutual conflagration brought about their chance meeting in that place at that particular time. But she had been wrong.

There had been no element of chance about Jake Farrell's plan—except perhaps the ease of it. He could hardly have expected his victim to deliver herself up, confused and vulnerable to his cynical manipulation. That had been luck—the devil's own luck. And, like a devil, he had exploited it to the full.

What happened in the glade had been no passionate accident. He had taken his chance, cold-bloodedly acting to sabotage the union that would spell the end of his hopes of inheritance. She had been nothing to him but a means to an end, their childhood friendship forgotten except as a tool for her own destruction.

Jake Farrell had been determined to destroy her marriage before it had even started. No wonder he had been so furious to discover that she planned to go through with the wedding.

It hadn't been love he had made to her, beneath the sentinel trees. It had been hate. And hate grew where it was planted.

He would have a cold night, waiting there on the spot where he had betrayed her. Amber smiled, bleakly. Just now, she hated Jake Farrell very much.

'Amber, I'm sorry. But I couldn't find it anywhere.' Sandra glanced quickly at the door of the bedroom as if to ensure that they weren't overheard. 'I looked where you said—in the clearing by the oak tree. And on the path. I found your shoes, by the way. And——' She flushed. 'And your slip. But the ring wasn't there.'

'Oh.' Her make-up forgotten, Amber sat down with a bump on the bed and stared blankly at her friend. 'Then what——? Sandra, it *must* have been there.'

'Well, if it was, I couldn't see it. Look, while you're away I'll get my brother to lend me his metal detector and go over the place properly. I mean, you're right—it must be there. Only you'll have to tell Simon——'

'I can't! Oh, Sandra, I——'

But at that moment the telephone bell rang, and Amber started immediately to her feet as her aunt bustled back into the room.

'Ignore that, Amber; your uncle will answer it. And watch what you're doing with that mascara, or you'll be walking down the aisle looking more like a zebra crossing than a bride.'

Right on cue, a downstairs door opened and the insistent ringing stopped abruptly. Amber tensed. What if...?

Her aunt leant forward and wiped an offending blotch from her cheek. 'Or possibly a panda, looking at those rings under your eyes. I presume you slept badly. Well, I told you it was ridiculous, staying up late the other night. "Hen party", indeed. As if a bride ever slept well the night before her wedding.' She stood back and surveyed her niece with compressed lips. 'You'll do. Now come on, quickly, and let Sandra do your hair.'

'Yes...' Amber struggled to tear her attention away from the half-heard sounds that floated up the stairs. But there was nothing she could do. If Jake phoned again, she would just have to hope that his pride, at least, would stop him saying anything incriminating to her uncle.

It was impossible now, on this day of all days, for her to hang over the phone. A bride on her wedding morning had more important concerns.

Her uncle called up the stairs with a message from the florist and Amber let out a breath she hadn't realised she was holding. She felt the tension that gripped her ease away, to be replaced by an irrational sense of something like disappointment. But that was absurd...

'I just wish he'd phone and get it over with,' she muttered privately as she put the finishing touches to her make-up. Her aunt looked enquiringly at her.

'Oh, nothing, Aunt Bella. Just yawning. You're right, I did find it difficult to sleep last night.' Amber peered at her reflection in the mirror and grimaced. Quite apart from the dark shadows above her cheekbones, the shade she had chosen did nothing to disguise the curious amber colour of her eyes. *Tiger-eyes*... Only he had ever called her that.

She glanced at her watch. Less than an hour to go; it was too late now to start redoing her make-up. 'What do you think, Sandra? Do I look all right?' Amber held her face up for inspection and listened with half an ear to the reassurance she knew would follow, then settled back to watch as her bridesmaid wielded the curling tongs in a vain attempt to tame her mane of hair.

She had been sure, somehow, that he would phone again. But after three more nerve-racking calls that turned out to be from the local hotel confirming details for the reception, a wrong number, and those of her colleagues at the travel agency who would not be attending the wedding ceremony, the hope—no, *fear*—had faded. The thought suddenly came to her that, soon, it would be too late...

'Come *on*, Amber. It's time for the dress.' Her aunt's brisk voice jerked Amber back to consciousness. What on earth was she thinking of, letting a cold, scheming devil like Jake Farrell get to her like this?

This is my wedding morning, she told herself sternly. This is me, getting ready to put on my dress. This is a very important moment in my life—and I don't want to spoil it by wondering if Jake Farrell is going to ring me up with another pack of lies...

Was it imagination or could she see the faintest suspicion of a tear on her aunt's rigid cheek? And Sandra looked flushed and sentimental as she held the white frothy wedding dress in readiness. So why was it that all the bride could think of was a voice on the end of the phone?

Amber slipped off her towelling bathrobe and raised her arms ready to slip into the dress. Aunt Bella frowned.

'You haven't put your engagement ring on yet, you silly girl. Do it now, or you'll forget.'

Amber felt her whole body blush as she tried not to look at Sandra. Damn! Why did Aunt Bella always have to notice these things...? 'No— I can't,' she improvised desperately. 'It's too loose—it wouldn't be safe. I might lose it.'

'Don't be ridiculous, Amber. You must wear it—today of all days. You'll just have to be careful. Where is it, Sandra?'

'Mrs Farrell, I—it—it's all my fault. When Amber gave me the ring the other night, I misunderstood—I thought she wanted me to take it into the jewellers to be adjusted. So I took it in this morning... I'm afraid it won't be ready for a few days.'

'Oh, really! Amber, how could you be so careless? That ring is a Family heirloom, and——'

'Mrs Farrell, I think the car will be here any minute.' Sandra stepped in diplomatically and Amber flashed her friend a smile of gratitude for her swift invention. Then, stepping forward, she allowed the sea of satin and lace to break over her head.

The cars arrived a few minutes later, just as they finished adjusting her veil. Mrs Farrell coughed and looked, for her, a little flustered— rather as if, Amber thought irreverently, she was about to lay an egg. Sandra slipped tactfully out of the room, leaving Amber alone with her aunt.

'You look very nice indeed, Amber, dear,' she said with unaccustomed kindness. 'Very suitable. I'm sure you'll make Simon a lovely wife.'

'Thank you, Auntie. I'll try to make him happy.' Oh, God, she thought, please let me make him happy. Suddenly she felt very cold. Please...

'I'm sure you will. You're a good girl at heart, Amber—not like your mother.' Mrs Farrell nodded with satisfaction, then looked around nervously and started to talk rather fast.

'And you're not worried about... about to-night, are you? I mean, I know that you young people are supposed to know everything these days, but . . .' She ground to an embarrassed halt.

Amber smiled, although inside she was feeling colder and colder, as though her life was bleeding away. 'Don't worry, Auntie. I know—everything I have to, I should think.'

'I suppose you do.'

There was disapproval in her voice, and Amber thought, I suppose she thinks Simon and I have slept together. And it suddenly hit her, the enormity of what she had done. Of what she was doing . . .

They were halfway down the drive to the waiting cars when the phone began to ring.

CHAPTER FOUR

HE WASN'T at the church. As she walked down the aisle on her uncle's arm, Amber was guiltily aware that she shouldn't even be thinking about Jake Farrell's presence or absence. Her eyes should have been modestly fixed on her bouquet of summer orchids, not flickering surreptitiously from side to side along the pews, looking for one lean brown face among the fancy hats and slicked-down hairstyles of the congregation.

Damn you, Jake Farrell! What have you done to me? Amber felt tears of anger prickle behind her eyes. This was her wedding-day. She should have been thinking about Simon, waiting for her by the altar—and instead, her mind was full of a man whose only motivation was a cruel self-interest. In a way, it was a worse betrayal than what had happened before...

As a tear broke free and trickled wetly down her cheek, Amber breathed an unaccustomed 'thank you' to her aunt for insisting on a traditional veil. At least no one could see her foolishness. And soon it would all be over. They would be married and she could forget that Jake Farrell had ever existed. Another tear joined the first and she had to steel herself not to brush it away. She need never see him again.

Never again... The trickle threatened to become a flood. Instinctively, she clutched at her uncle's grey-suited arm for support and felt an answering squeeze. Somehow, the gesture gave her the strength to continue. It wasn't just Simon she would be failing, but her uncle and aunt as well. As her mother had failed them . . . They all trusted her. She couldn't let them down.

Concentrate on the music, she told herself grimly, trying to lose herself in the organ's soaring notes. Another ten steps. How far was it, for goodness' sake? It felt more like Westminster Abbey than a little parish church. But at last she was standing beside Simon and the music had stopped. And there was nothing to hear but the faint rustling of the congregation and the solemnly nasal voice of the rector as he began to pronounce the service.

'Dearly beloved, we are gathered together here in the sight of God, and in the face of this congregation, to join together . . .'

The heavy oak door at the back of the church creaked open and then slammed shut, sending a ripple of disturbance through the anticipatory quiet. Amber felt Simon shift uneasily beside her and for the first time it occurred to her that perhaps he too was nervous. She had been too tied up in her own worries to even consider that he might also be suffering from pre-wedding nerves.

The rector frowned, coughed, and returned pointedly to his text. '. . . to join together this Man and this Woman in holy Matrimony; which is an honourable estate . . .'

Was it her imagination, or had the background rustling intensified with the interruption? And it had been joined by a low murmur of comment, too quiet for her to hear the words, but loud enough to make her ears strain to catch it. Like the distant humming of bees...

'...and therefore is not by any to be enterprised, nor taken in hand, unadvisedly, lightly, or wantonly, to satisfy men's carnal lusts and appetites, like brute beasts that have no understanding...'

Beneath her veil, Amber felt her face redden, as if the rector's ancient words had been written afresh for her. For a moment, she found herself wondering wildly if perhaps he knew; if perhaps he were going to denounce her——

The humming was louder now, almost a disturbance, and, glancing up, she could see the rector's eyes flicker with annoyance. A memory came from nowhere, of standing on a station platform, waiting for her mother to return from one of her trips. The station-master had taken her into his office and there had been a small wooden box labelled 'Danger! Bees in Transit'. And when Amber had daringly put her ear close to it, she had heard the angry beating of a thousand wings.

She remembered it now; that sound of contained aggression; of anger. The people behind her were *angry*... It didn't make sense. What was there to be angry about at a wedding? The temptation to turn and look was almost unbearable.

'...both in prosperity and adversity. Into which holy estate these two persons present come now to be joined. Therefore if any man can shew any just cause, why they may not lawfully be joined together, let him now speak, or else hereafter for ever hold his peace.'

There was a brief pause when all the rustling stopped; that moment of tenseness in even the best regulated of marriage ceremonies when everyone present held their breath and wondered for a second what would happen if...

Only this time it wasn't necessary to wonder.

This time, a man stood up.

There was a gasp from the congregation, and Amber's control broke. She cast a terrified glance behind her, but she already knew what she would see. Jake Farrell's dark figure strode from the back of the church, incongruously dressed in the same leather jacket and jeans that she had seen him in at lunch the previous day. The thought came to her that perhaps he had slept in them, there in the glade. Waiting for her...

His chin was unshaven and there was a wildness about him. 'This has gone far enough, Amber. You're coming with me.'

Only a rough edge to his voice betrayed him, though Amber wasn't sure that anyone else would have known. His self-control was total, but she seemed to have developed extra antennae where Jake Farrell was concerned. With a shock of fear, she realised that he had been drinking. 'Alcohol just strips away the layer of civilisation in us...' His own words came vividly back to her, and she could see the truth of them in his face.

'Jake, no...' But her whispered words were a prayer with no hope of an answer and she shrank back fearfully, knowing the danger she was in.

Her movement seemed to be the catalyst the situation had been waiting for.

'What the hell's going on?' Simon stepped forward belligerently. 'What do you think you're doing, barging in here——?'

'Come with me, Amber.' It was as if Jake didn't even notice the other man's existence. 'Come with me now, and it will all be over. Don't make me hurt you any more.'

'I can't.' But his eyes were drawing her magnetically towards him, and she felt her feet move. There was a cliff before her, and a part of her wanted nothing more than to step with him over the edge. Somewhere in the background, she could hear her aunt's outraged protests, and the rector's voice high with genteel panic as he tried to guide them into the vestry. Hands pulled at her; noise buffeted her. But she couldn't move.

'You must. Or I shall make you.'

She didn't ask how. Somehow, standing there, he seemed invincible—like the pivot of the world. It didn't occur to her to doubt that he could carry out his threat.

'I——' She was teetering on the brink. And then another voice broke through the maelstrom.

'You! It was you she met in the woods! The other night . . .' From her position as maid-of-honour, Sandra suddenly threw herself at the intruder, an avenging fury in peach satin, her nails clawing his face. 'It was you who attacked her . . .'

It was as if the air in the church suddenly froze. 'Oh, Amber, I shouldn't have let you walk back alone . . .' Sandra broke into uncontrollable sobs and Simon put his arm round her and led her gently away. But Amber was oblivious to their going. She couldn't drag her eyes away from Jake.

'So that's what you told them.' His words pierced her like a blade of ice.

'Jake, I——' She wanted to deny it, to tell him ... To tell him what? Her mind was numb and her tongue seemed frozen in her head. All she could think of was that she had to explain ...

His eyes had gone curiously dead, as if a steel shutter had come down behind them. A trickle of blood ran down one cheek, but he showed no signs of noticing it. Amber felt an overpowering desire to reach up and wipe it away.

But as she moved, Jake's hand jerked towards the inner pocket of his jacket and she flinched, knowing instinctively from that clumsy, involuntary movement that he was at the very edge of his control.

'So I attacked you, did I?' By some mysterious agreement, a hush fell over the church. All eyes were fixed on the drama being played out before them. Even her uncle's and the rector's voice were silent, as if they recognised the inevitability of what was happening.

From inside his jacket, Jake pulled out something small that flashed and glittered in the light. Like a spark of the same cold fire that burned in his eyes.

'Then you'd better have the proof.' His hand flew out and the spark of ice rolled and bounced across the stone flags of the floor between them. It seemed to take a long time to come to rest at her feet. There was no longer any doubting what it was and a hiss of horrified recognition ran through the church.

Without a word, Jake turned and strode back down the aisle. Nobody stopped him. His part was finished and the eyes moved on. To Simon, who watched with eyes bulging with outrage as his cousin stormed past the pew where he had settled Sandra to recover from her sobbing.

The slamming of the heavy oak door seemed to jolt him back into life. 'Amber?' Simon's face was a picture of pompous bewilderment, and, for a moment, it was as if she was seeing it for the first time. A pale, young, rather vacuous face... A face totally unsuited to the drama in which it now played a part.

'I think you owe me an explanation,' he added uncertainly. 'What's going on? How did Jake get your ring? I thought... You told me...'

He stepped towards her, and it came to her that the expression on his face was not pain, or anguish, but social outrage. And in that second, Amber knew that it could all be all right. She could blame it on Jake—claim he was drunk—and they could carry on with the wedding.

Whatever she said, Simon would believe—even the loss of her engagement ring she could somehow explain away. Because he wanted to believe her. Because, whatever his private doubts, what his conventional soul most shrank from was a scene...

She could lie to him, and Aunt Bella would back her up, and the interruption would be put down to Jake Farrell's last-ditch attempts to share in his grandfather's inheritance. It would be a nine-day wonder in the village. But eventually people would forget.

She had only to lie. Simon wanted her to lie. The blood pounded in her head and her lips seemed dry and cracked as she opened her mouth.

'What Sandra said . . . it wasn't true. We did— we did meet. But he didn't attack me.' Her voice was almost inaudible. 'I'm sorry, Simon. I can't marry you. I think I'd better go home.'

And in the ensuing uproar, all she could see was the look of astonishment on his face.

She could still see it in her mind's eye three days later, when she stepped off the small plane which had carried her the final step from Jakarta to Bali. They should have been arriving here together . . .

Once again, she wondered if she had done the right thing by coming alone on the trip which would have been her honeymoon. But at the time her only desire had been to get away. Away from her aunt's fury and contempt. Away from the shame which had kept her a prisoner in her room, afraid to go downstairs or answer the phone. Away from the memories . . .

So, when she had remembered the tickets in her going-away bag, it had seemed like an answer to prayer. She had carefully repacked her luggage, this time omitting the clothes and accessories that Simon had bought her. It didn't leave much, but, since she was travelling alone, that would be all to the good. And then she had gone downstairs and called for a taxi before telling her uncle and stony-faced aunt of her decision.

They had made no attempt to hide their relief, although her uncle had at least tried to check that she was adequately provided for for the journey. Her aunt had made no such concessions.

'And on your return, no doubt you will be making other arrangements,' she had added coldly. 'You can hardly expect to continue living under this roof. I will have your belongings packed up and then communication between us will cease. Your mother's behaviour has already stained the reputation of this Family—and evidently you are determined to go the same sordid way.'

The words had cut Amber to the heart, but she had said nothing. What was there to say? It was true, after all. And nothing her aunt could say to her could plumb the depths of her own self-hatred. She had ruined everything, and now all she wanted to do was crawl away and hide.

At the airport, she had checked in her luggage and then steeled herself to do what she had been putting off ever since the wedding. She had to write to Simon. If only she could explain... But the words wouldn't come. She didn't feel she knew any more what would make him feel better or worse. How could you write to a man who had turned into a stranger?

So in the end, the note she had sent him had said very little. Only that she was sorry, and that the fault had been hers and not Jake's. She had sealed and stamped the envelope and dropped it into the post-box before she could have second thoughts.

And then she had walked through the gate to Departures. Leaving her life behind her.

But now, as she walked down the steps of the plane on to the hot tarmac, she felt her spirits lift. This was a whole new world; a world where her sins could not follow her. Even the air was different: thicker, heavier, with a faint sweet smell of cloves. Above all, it was hotter. The heat distorted the view across the terminal, making the green palm trees around the perimeter waver and shift.

She could feel the weight of it on her shoulders, tiring her like an additional burden as she carried her hand-luggage across the dusty concrete. In the airport buildings, the spicy smell intensified, making her tired senses swim with the odour of burning incense.

She went through the formalities in a daze. At Passport Control she forgot at first to answer to the name of 'Farrell' on her newly altered documents, and this further reminder of what might have been dulled her mood of expectation with an ache of regret. But at last she emerged from the stuffy interior with her small suitcase. And stepped into a world of noise and vivid, jostling colours.

Amber began to feel a little overwhelmed. She hadn't slept well now for days, and the long flight had left her exhausted, and ill-equipped to deal with all the practical difficulties of a lone traveller.

Standing still for a moment to find her bearings, she was soon helplessly surrounded by drivers of taxis, little open buses and even horse-drawn buggies, all clamouring for the privilege of transporting her. But just as she was about to pick one at random, she was amazed to hear someone calling her name.

'Nona Amber? Nona Amber?' A small man appeared behind her, from the terminal building. His smiling Balinese face was scarcely higher than her own, but he swept the luggage from her hands with practised skill.

'You no go with these men.' Temporarily redepositing her luggage on the ground, he turned, waving his hands and shouting incomprehensibly at the little crowd that had gathered until it melted away. 'I Pak Ketut. You call me Ketut. And you Nona Amber...Ashley?' He stumbled a little over the last word.

Presumably he had been sent by the hotel to collect her. She nodded, and was rewarded with another friendly beam. 'I drive you to hotel,' Ketut said with a little bow. 'Is all arrange. I very sorry not to find you in airport, but I cannot find this name on flight-list. ''Ash-ley'', is this correct? Have I made a mistake?'

'No, that's right.' The little man looked so worried that she felt she had to explain the mix-up. 'The tickets were booked in the name of Farrell.' If anything that seemed to puzzle him even more, so she added in explanation, 'My fiancé's name.'

Her guide's face cleared. 'Ah! You are married now. Ash-ley virgin name, yes?'

Amber opened her mouth to correct his misapprehension, then shut it again. What did it matter, after all? Her passport proclaimed her to be Mrs Farrell, and all the arrangements were made in Simon's name. In fact, thinking about it, she was surprised the hotel had had her maiden name at all—but probably she had given it without thinking when she made the booking.

Besides, just at that moment, she felt she wouldn't have minded being addressed as Napoleon Bonaparte if it meant getting out of this heat and into a lovely cool bed... She followed her saviour out to his vehicle, one of the small open trucks she had noticed earlier. It was fitted with seats for about eight people, but she was its only occupant.

As he drove, Ketut lit up a cigarette and Amber recognised the clove-like smell which had pervaded the airport. 'Is all arrange,' he repeated, looking back at her and waving his cigarette expansively. 'Your husband, he say to look after you good.'

'My husband!' Amber started up in her seat, then sat down quickly as the little truck crashed at high speed over a pothole. 'You've talked to Sim—I mean, Mr Farrell?'

'On telephone, yes. Mr Farrell big man in travel business; he give me plenty work. So when he say you come here alone, he ask me to take care of you.' The note of puzzlement came back into his voice. 'But he no say you his wife. He say, "Ashley". In England, wife take husband name, yes?'

'Well, usually.' That solved one mystery at least; if Simon had arranged for Ketut to meet her, that explained why he had been asking for her under her own name. No one knew better than Simon that she had no right to call herself Farrell... And yet he had felt kindly enough towards her to arrange all this... 'It's rather complicated, Ketut. Just call me Amber and don't worry—oh!'

Ketut swerved violently to avoid a scrawny chicken which had picked that moment to wander across the road, turning round as he did so to smile reassurance at his passenger. Amber found herself wishing fervently that he would either keep his eyes on the road or else slow down to a less bone-shattering pace.

But he seemed to drive by instinct rather than sight. 'You here one month, yes?' Amber nodded distractedly, her eyes fixed on a bicycle wobbling along the road in front of them, weighed down by sheaves of vegetables that completely obscured the rider from view.

'You want see temple, see *odalan*, see volcano; I take you.' Without taking his eyes off Amber's face, or his hand off the horn, Ketut wrenched the wheel round to avoid what had seemed like an inevitable collision. 'Is all arrange. No pay. You want buy souvenir, you tell me. I speak Balinese language good; make good bargain. Yes?'

'Oh, yes, thank you.' After the way she had treated him, Amber had mixed feelings about accepting Simon's generous gesture. But it would hurt him still more if she refused—and a refusal would hurt Ketut as well. And besides, the little Balinese's help would be invaluable. She had been worried about travelling alone.

A warm rush of gratitude towards Simon for his thoughtfulness swept over her, bringing in its wake a wave of sadness. Was he very unhappy? Perhaps she had been fooling herself in believing that he would see her desertion as no more than a social embarrassment...

If only things had been different. If only she hadn't met Jake that night in the glade. If only he hadn't decided to sacrifice her to his own greed. And if only her mother's passionate blood hadn't betrayed her...

But, despite her wishing, Amber knew she had done the right thing. Whatever his motives for saying so, Jake had been right. You couldn't go back. It had been too late for her and Simon from the moment Jake had taken her in his arms... She had been mad to think she could cope with living a lie.

'This your hotel.' The truck screeched to a stop outside a low building with an ornately carved roof and exterior. Amber thought it looked more like a temple than a hotel. Inside, the air-conditioning was cool and welcoming, making her realise just how hot and dirty she felt.

To her relief, Ketut dealt swiftly with all the check-in arrangements before accompanying her out to her 'room'—which turned out to be a little palm-thatched bungalow set in the hotel's luxuriant gardens.

Inside, it was divided into two rooms, the larger dominated by a huge king-size bed while the sitting-room had two armchairs and a bed-settee which Ketut proceeded to demonstrate. He showed off the accommodation with as much

pride as if he had built it himself, while Amber
yawned and eyed the bed and the shower in the
little bathroom with a covetous eye.

'Tomorrow we go see temple, yes? In afternoon?' Amber nodded, and they made arrangements to meet at Reception. When the little man
left, she felt that his friendly chatter had been all
that had kept her awake.

After a hurried shower, she fell, still damp, into
the welcoming bed. Outside, the incessant
chirping of insects formed a constant background to the more distant sounds of music and
laughter.

Amber lay for a few minutes, savouring the
exotic sounds and scents that wafted through the
woven walls. Then she drifted, exhausted, into a
mercifully dreamless sleep.

CHAPTER FIVE

OVER the next week, Amber's life became attuned to the languorous rhythms of the island, her timetable regulated by the sun and the sea. With no need of an alarm clock, she woke in the fresh early morning, to enjoy the few hours of coolness before the heat of the day.

Then, while the tide was in on the long, white-sanded beach, she swam and lazed around, drinking deliciously refreshing fruit drinks from the beach bars or wandering up into the hotel gardens to pick ripe fruit from the trees which lined the paths.

At Ketut's suggestion, she had spent some of her *rupiahs* on a face-mask and snorkel. It turned out to be a small price to pay for the hours of pleasure she enjoyed in the clear blue underwater world. And then she let herself be persuaded into an exhilarating ride on a *prahu*—an outrigger canoe belonging to one of Ketut's contacts.

'Oh, this is wonderful!' The *prahu* with its triangular sail shot with intoxicating speed over the clear water, like an exotic dragonfly on its long splayed legs. Amber had to gasp to catch her breath. It was like drinking the wind—and the draught was stronger than any wine.

Seeing her enjoyment, the grinning steersman hauled in on the sail until it seemed as though they were skimming above the waves rather than on them and Amber was forced to cling with both hands to the wooden thwarts. She felt the wind catch her hair, ripping it free from its careful pleat and licking her face with tongues of bright sea-flame. But she made no attempt to tie it back. For the first time in years, she found herself laughing aloud with delight.

It was like a return to Eden. And when the blue line of the sea retreated into the distance, leaving banks of bright coral exposed, she explored the island in Ketut's *bemo*. Despite its battered appearance, the little truck proved capable of dealing with the steepest gradients and sharpest bends as they climbed and twisted among the steeply terraced rice fields and luxuriant coconut groves.

With her guide's enthusiastic assistance, Amber supplemented her wardrobe by shopping in the local markets, buying sarongs and traditional blouses that she now wore in preference to her heavy Western clothes. The batik cotton the islanders wore was beautiful, and ideal for the climate, protecting her sensitive skin from the sun and yet cool and light.

And if its soft touch reminded her of other caresses, of the warmth of male flesh through silk, and the heat of male lips—then she would dive a little deeper, swim harder, drive further. And the memories would fade again, until at last Jake's dark face, and the cruelty with which he had treated her, seemed less real than the spirits and demons that inhabited the lush Balinese countryside.

As well as increasing her comfort, her new clothes made Amber feel more a part of the local scene. Often on their travels, once she had made it clear that she had no objection, Ketut would stop at a waved signal to pick up a group of women walking to or from a market along the dusty island roads. They would crowd into the *bemo*, chattering and giggling, pleased to be saving the few *rupiahs* the trip would normally cost. It gave Amber a chance to experiment with the few words of Indonesian she had learned. Her efforts delighted them, and she envied them their unselfconscious beauty and easy grace.

Many of the women, even the youngest, carried a baby perched on one hip, and Ketut explained that children under six months old were considered sacred because of their purity. They were never allowed to touch the ground, being carried constantly by their mother, or by an older sister or aunt.

Certainly they seemed to thrive on the loving attention, and scarcely ever cried. Amber made Ketut teach her the words for 'pretty baby'— *'anak cantik'*—and found this was usually enough to get a plump, gurgling infant bestowed on her with pride for the rest of the trip. But her pleasure was tinged with sadness. If only... In a year's time, it might have been her own child she was holding. But now Jake Farrell had torn those dreams to shreds.

In the evenings, when Ketut returned to his family, Amber was left at the hotel. She ate from the sumptuous buffet table and watched the exhibitions of traditional dancing and gamelangong music staged for guests, or wandered out on to the little town's sinuous main street to explore the shops and restaurants.

It was then, without her guide's cheerful companionship, that it was most difficult to keep the emptiness at bay. But, if she was lonely, she was aware that it was a self-chosen penance. It was high season for tourism, and many of the other guests in the hotel were English-speaking and disposed to be friendly.

As a woman alone, Amber found that she attracted her share of male attention—so much so that she soon came to be grateful for the fact that she was known in the hotel by her 'married' name, despite the discomfort it caused her to be addressed as 'Mrs Farrell' by the staff or other guests.

Without her ever giving an explanation, it seemed to have become accepted that she was waiting for her husband, who had been held up on business. Amber didn't correct the story. At least it made it easier to fend off the holiday Lotharios' sometimes determined attempts on her solitude.

At mealtimes, she sat alone, taking a wry amusement in picking out the honeymoon couples; the ones with whom she and Simon would have become friendly in the normal course of events. But she instinctively shied away from anything more than the most casual contact. She sensed that her bubble of enchantment might not survive too close a reminder of what might have been.

She was content to have achieved a fragile happiness. But then something happened that shattered that contentment for good.

It was Ketut who delivered the blow, running excitedly from the Reception building where he had gone to collect her key on return from one of their afternoon expeditions.

'Is good news!' he beamed, as he hurried to join her on the path. 'Man say your husband here. So now you have proper honeymoon, yes?'

'What? Ketut, are you sure they didn't mean someone else? I haven't got—I mean, it can't be my husband. They must have made a mistake.'

But the little man was adamant that the message had been for Mrs Farrell. 'Your husband; he here now. He wait in room, so no key.' He gestured with empty hands, as if the absence of the key was in itself proof. 'He arrive this afternoon.' He beamed again. 'You very happy now. Tomorrow, perhaps you not need me, yes? You stay with husband?'

'No—yes—oh, I don't know, Ketut. Perhaps I could leave a message at Reception?' Amber's mind was refusing to function, as if she had suddenly been caught up in a dream which wasn't even hers. Simon—here in Bali? Like Aladdin rubbing the lamp, she had conjured an imaginary husband and he had appeared...

'Yes, of course.' Still smiling with delight at what he presumably imagined was her happy confusion, Ketut put his hands together in the prayer-like gesture of greeting and gave a little bow. '*Selamat tinggal*, Nyonya Amber. Goodbye.

Give my respect to your husband. I hope to see you again soon.'

'Yes, thank you. Goodbye, Ketut.' She searched distractedly for the correct response. *'Selamat jalan.'* And then at last, he was walking back to the *bemo*. And she was alone.

All the way to the bungalow, Amber's benumbed brain was trying to come to terms with the new situation. If Simon was here, what did that mean? That he had forgiven her? But how could any man forgive what she had done to him—especially Simon, who had inherited so much of his mother's pride? The full horror of that scene in the church came rushing back to her. He couldn't still want her after that. It wasn't possible.

Surely he couldn't? But, if not, why had he come? Somehow she couldn't see him in the role of avenging fury—unlike his cousin. If it had been Jake she had jilted, she could well believe that he would follow her to the ends of the earth to exact revenge. But Simon...it didn't ring true. Unbelievable as it seemed, he must have decided to forgive his errant bride.

She was almost at the bungalow now, and she could see the woven shutters drawn across the bedroom window to shut out the late afternoon sun. That morning she had opened them... It was true, then. Simon was here. Her 'husband' had arrived to claim her.

Only she no longer wanted him...

The realisation stopped her in her tracks, but at some deeper level the knowledge didn't come as a surprise. It was as if it had been growing within her, forced, like the lush vegetation, by the tropical sun. And now it had burst into flower...

She stared at the blank windows, trying to master the panic which rose within her. What was wrong with her? She should have been running joyfully to meet him, full of thankfulness that Jake's cruelty had not ruined their lives after all; not feeling that she would like to turn tail and flee in the opposite direction.

But he was here, and she couldn't run away. Whatever happened, he deserved that from her. They had to talk. And she could only hope that, when it came to it, she would somehow know what to say.

Taking a deep breath to steady herself, Amber pushed at the door, only realising as it swung open how much she had hoped to find it locked. The room was cool and dark, and for a moment she could see nothing. Then she heard a sigh from the direction of the bedroom. The door between was open, and she saw the bedcovers move.

Resisting the temptation to postpone the confrontation and leave her 'husband' to sleep, Amber quietly pulled back the shutter a few inches to let in some light, then tiptoed up to the bed and gently shook the heavily breathing mound under the sheet.

'Simon? Simon, it's me, Amber.' She shook him again. 'Wake up, darling—oh!'

In a moment, Amber's scream was cut off as her visitor leapt up to clamp his hand hard over her mouth. 'Shut up, you little fool. Do you want to get your "husband" thrown out?'

Her husband... But it wasn't Simon's blond hair that curled on the wrist that filled her vision. And it wasn't his voice that bit like acid into her consciousness.

It was Jake Farrell who held her contemptuously in his grasp. And, as she struggled ineffectually to free herself, Amber realised in horror that he was completely naked. The heat of his body seemed to burn her through the flimsy sarong, and, appallingly, she felt a tremor of excitement at the touch.

The surge of self-disgust that ran through her gave her courage and she sunk her teeth hard into the hand that gagged her. To her satisfaction, Jake let go with a gasp of pain, and she pulled herself free and turned to face him.

'That's just what I do want!' she flared. 'Isn't it enough for you to persecute me in England without following me out here as well? You've got what you wanted, damn you. Now I just want to be left alone.'

'Oh, yes, I can see that.' His voice was silky with an anger that Amber didn't understand. What right had he to be angry? 'I can see that, "Mrs Farrell". After all, you wouldn't want anyone to disturb your reunion with your *darling* Simon. You really are determined to get your claws into my little cousin, aren't you, Tigereyes?'

His eyes gleamed cruelly as he taunted her with the old nickname. 'But I'm afraid you've overestimated your power,' he went on with deliberate spite. 'Last time I saw him, your ex-fiancé was being very capably comforted by that harpy that attacked me in the church. What's her name—Sandra? She always was sweet on him, I seem to remember. Though God knows why.'

His hand went reflectively to his cheek and Amber could still see the long score where Sandra's fingers had raked him.

'I don't believe you,' Amber whispered. 'Anyway, why are you here? You can't hurt me any more, Jake. What do you want with me?'

'What would any husband want with such a delectable wife? Especially on his honeymoon?'

His eyes dropped for a moment, and Amber's involuntarily followed them, to be faced with the shocking evidence that she hadn't been alone in finding their struggle physically arousing.

She backed away from him, her eyes fixed determinedly on his face. 'Jake, put some clothes on, please,' she begged. Her anger was muted now by real fear. 'You can't stay here.'

'It's a little late for shyness, isn't it—"Mrs Farrell"? We are on honeymoon, after all.' But to her relief he picked up one of the sarongs which lay folded on a chair beside the bed and wrapped it around his waist. Even in her panic, she noticed that he kilted it as a *sarong pria*—the correct way, as Ketut had shown her, for a man. He had been to Bali before...

His voice was still mocking her. 'And as for not staying here—I'm booked in; the hotel were expecting me. They've even provided a complimentary bottle of champagne.'

Jake gestured at the table behind them and Amber saw that a bottle was indeed cooling in an ice-bucket next to a tray with two glasses. 'So perhaps I should pour us both a glass to celebrate?' His eyes caught and held hers with contempt and the temperature in the room seemed to drop by several degrees. 'And then you can explain to me just what the hell you were planning.'

Half mesmerised into obedience, half grateful for any move that promised to defuse the heart-stopping intimacy of their present situation, Amber stood back and watched as her visitor uncorked the waiting bottle with one economical twist and filled the glasses.

Silently, Jake held one out to her, and just as silently she took it. The tension seemed to stretch like a cord between them, until she wanted to scream to break it. But she fought back the panicky impulse. And at last he spoke, his voice rasping with the anger she still didn't understand.

'So tell me, "Mrs Farrell",' he said with deadly emphasis. 'How did you plan to get my cousin out here? And how did you propose to make your "darling Simon" forget what a faithless little bitch he'd got himself mixed up with? Apart from offering him that delectable body of yours, of course. Or did you think that would be enough?'

He ran his eyes over her with negligent contempt and Amber flushed as hotly as if she were naked under his gaze.

'I don't have the faintest idea what you're talking about, Jake,' she threw back defiantly. Somehow she managed to keep the tremor out of her voice. 'I wasn't planning anything. I just came out here to get away.'

'And just happened to call yourself "Mrs Farrell"? A name to which, I hardly ought to need remind you, you have no earthly right. And just happened to tell the hotel staff that your husband was delayed on business and would be joining you in a few days?'

'I didn't...'

But he cut her off harshly. 'Don't bother to lie. When I arrived at Reception and tried to book in as "Mr Farrell", they greeted me like a long-lost relative—and told me my wife was out sight-seeing but would be delighted that I had finally joined her. And I saw your passport, and your signature on the registration slip. You didn't leave much to chance, did you?'

He took a slow sip of his drink, but from his expression it could have been vinegar rather than wine. 'What were you going to do, Amber? Phone him long distance and weep crocodile tears into his ear?'

'No, I wasn't! And if you'd listen to me for more than two seconds, Jake Farrell, I could tell you——'

As her voice rose, Amber felt all the anger and distress that she had buried inside her since the wedding come flooding back, drowning her fear of the man who stood before her, accusing.

'Damn you! What right have you to come storming in here and questioning me like this?' she flared. Why should she justify herself to this man? 'What are you doing here, anyway? At least this was supposed to be my honeymoon; it was never yours.'

'That's very true. But I do seem to have rather hijacked it, don't I? A honeymoon is a game for two players, after all. And I can hardly go back to Reception now and explain that I'm not the husband you were waiting for. That would really confuse them.'

'Well, you can't stay here.' Amber looked at the bed with its rumpled sheets and felt another twinge of fear—mixed with another emotion that she shied away from identifying. Surely he couldn't mean...? She gripped the stem of her champagne glass with both hands to stop the shaking that threatened to betray her. 'If you stay, then I'll go, Jake. You can't force me——'

'Oh, but I can.' There was something in his tone of quiet menace that stopped her defiance in its tracks. An air of certainty... 'I am your husband, after all—"Mrs Farrell",' he went on. 'And so, naturally, the desk staff were happy to return your passport to me. I've put it with my own—for safe-keeping. I didn't think you would be needing it for a while.'

It took a few seconds for the enormity of what he was saying to sink in. Without a passport she wouldn't be able to leave the island—or check into another hotel. She wouldn't even be able to change her remaining traveller's cheques. She was as much Jake Farrell's prisoner as if he had bound her hand and foot.

'You bastard!' Amber felt her last threads of self-control snap under the tension. Hardly knowing what she did, she flung the untouched contents of her glass into that dark, sardonic face. But the momentary pleasure she felt to see his eyes blink in pain was soon wiped out by her fear at the savage response she had unleashed.

'You little bitch!' Jake lunged at her, more quickly than she would have thought a man his size could move. And, hampered by the folds of her sarong, she had no chance to escape. Before she knew what was happening, he had picked her up bodily and thrown her on to the bed, kneeling over her and holding her helpless with her hands above her head. His thumbs bit into her wrists.

'Don't you ever do that to me again,' he ground. 'Or I'll make you drink the whole bottle. And we both know how much resistance you'd put up after that, don't we, "Mrs Farrell"? Personally, I preferred you the way you were the other night. You were a lot more tractable.'

'Oh!' Grimly, Amber fought to free herself; twisting and kicking beneath his weight, but in vain. The only effect of her struggle was to loosen the knot which held her sarong in place and, feeling it slipping from her waist, she was forced to abandon such direct efforts.

The last thing she needed now was to inflame him even more. Her position was precarious enough as it was. Instead, she let herself go limp. 'Let go of me, Jake,' she warned. 'Or I'll scream the place down.'

He shrugged with apparent unconcern. 'Go ahead.' Transferring both her wrists to one broad hand, he reached out with the other for the champagne bottle which still stood on the table by the bed. 'But don't expect me not to try and stop you.' And, tilting the bottle with the delicacy of a wine-waiter, he let a thin trickle of the bubbling liquid run out and over her face.

Her first scream was quite involuntary, as the stinging effervescence touched her eyes. The second was a deliberate production, as he tilted the bottle further and the trickle became a steady stream. Surely someone would come? The hotel boasted in its literature of the high ratio of staff to every guest. So how come there was no one around when she needed them?

'Stop it! Stop that, you—ah!' And then her protests were drowned in champagne, and she was forced to swallow and keep her mouth firmly shut if his threat to make her drink the whole bottle wasn't to be fulfilled there and then.

'What's the matter? Don't you like champagne? Not that this is a particularly good year, but it has its uses.' With infuriating calmness, he slowed the flow again to a trickle, and Amber breathed a sigh of relief.

But her respite was short-lived. To her horror, she felt the stinging coldness trail from her face to her neck and downwards, spilling over the thin cotton blouse that was all that covered her bra-less breasts.

As the stream hit her nipples, first one and then, with artistic precision, the other, Amber gasped and twisted beneath Jake's pinioning weight. She felt her sarong slip further down her hips but it was impossible to ignore the fizzing, buzzing sensation that almost drove her mad.

Her face was still wet with the wine, and she couldn't open her eyes, but she didn't need to see to know what sort of spectacle she was presenting. The blouse had ridden up high under her tormented breasts and the flimsy cotton was plastered to her writhing flesh. She flushed with shame to feel her nipples harden under the relentless downpour.

But her humiliation and anger were rapidly being submerged under a different kind of emotion. And as the stream left her breasts to spill down over her stomach, and the neat triangle of cotton her sarong had fallen to expose, she heard herself gasp again and arch against him with involuntary desire.

'Mind—don't waste it.' His voice sounded different; huskier; thicker. 'It would be a pity to spill such a precious cup.' And before she could wonder what he meant, she felt his mouth warm on the wine-cooled skin of her navel, and his tongue, drinking the pool of champagne that had collected there. His grip had loosened on her wrists, but Amber was past any thoughts of flight; past anything except the exquisite sensations that emanated from that flickering tongue.

She moaned with pleasure, and his mouth moved upwards over her cool, wet skin. Once more the wine baptised her breast. And then, with preternatural sensitivity, she felt the warmth of his breath as Jake approached to taste this new libation. But scarcely had his lips touched her when a sound outside galvanised her back into action.

There was a knock on the outer door, then the rattle of a key in the lock. Amber leapt up, scrabbling clumsily at her sarong to refasten it.

'Your laundry, Mrs Farrell. You want to check?' The room-boy's cheerful voice was almost on them, and she froze, staring at Jake in panic. To her relief, he took charge, grabbing a sarong and striding out into the sitting-room to stop the boy in his tracks.

'I'll take that. Don't bother about checking it; we'll accept the hotel's count.' His voice was grim again, having lost the husky gentleness it had had only moments before. 'And ask housekeeping to send the chambermaid round with fresh sheets, please. My wife has had an accident with the champagne.'

Amber heard the rustle of a banknote as a tip changed hands, and listened with illogical resentment to the boy's effusive thanks. How dared Jake blame it on her?

But that anger was second to the fury she felt at herself. Once more, forgetting his self-interested motives, she had delivered herself as a willing victim into Jake Farrell's hands. And she was further than ever from escaping his relentless pursuit.

CHAPTER SIX

HE WOULD be back at any second.

Acting on pure adrenalin, without any clear idea of what she expected to happen next, Amber dived into the bathroom and bolted the door. Now at least there was a barrier between them. It wasn't a very solid barrier, but it was better than nothing. Leaning back against the door as if to add her own weight to her defences, she stared into the mirror opposite and wondered what to do.

Her own reflection stared back at her. At first she didn't take it in, but when she did she felt her stomach tighten again with fear. Because it was a stranger who looked back at her from the mirror; a woman whose wildly disordered hair flamed in a halo of tempestuous fire around her head. A woman whose cheeks were still flushed with desire...

A woman whose blouse was half torn open at the front, the wet cotton clinging to every contour with such erotic accuracy that plain nudity would have been more decorous.

Amber stared at her reflection and knew that this was the real enemy she had to fight. Not the man she could hear moving angrily around the room behind her, knocking the lightweight bamboo furniture around like a bull on the rampage, but this woman who dissolved into

molten lava at his touch, against sense and against
reason. This passionate woman...

She was an enemy no barriers could hold back.
And Amber felt a shiver of fear.

Something—perhaps the champagne bottle—
crashed to the floor, and she heard Jake swear
briefly and vividly before resuming his pacing.
But then the tension seemed to get too much for
him, and she felt the door shudder against her
back as he pounded it with his fist.

'What the hell are you doing in there, woman?'

Amber said nothing, hoping against all
reasonable hope that he might give up and go
away. But she should have known better. The
thunder came again.

'You can't hide in there forever,' he yelled.
'What do you think is going to happen? If you're
hoping I'll leave, Tiger-eyes, you'd better prepare
for a disappointment. I've got the bed out here,
and access to room-service—which is more than
I had last week, waiting for you in that damn
wood. What are you going to do, eat the soap?
However long you stall, I'll still be here. So you
might as well come out and talk about this.'

'Talk!' The injustice of it stirred Amber to
speech. 'So far, I haven't noticed you doing much
talking,' she shouted back. 'Or listening. Why
don't you try behaving like a human being for a
while, Jake Farrell, instead of some kind of
walking volcano? Then perhaps I might come
out. Though not,' she hastily amended as she
glimpsed herself once more in the mirror, 'until
I've had a shower and changed.' If he saw her
again in this state...

But at last the hammering ceased. 'All right, then! I'm listening! And it had better be good. Or I'll break the bloody door down.'

'Oh, very reasonable.' But she took care to keep her muttered comment too quiet for Jake to hear. 'I don't know why you're here, Jake. I don't know what the hell you think gives you the right to any explanations from me. But since you seem to have got it into your head that I'm planning some sort of come-back, you can set your mind at rest. After what you did last week, Simon wouldn't marry me if I were the last woman on earth.'

There was a short silence on the other side of the door. 'So you do realise that, then,' Jake said in a more normal voice. 'Then what was the point of this "Mrs Farrell" business?' The threatening note began to reassert itself, and he banged the door for emphasis. 'Just wishful thinking?'

'No! Honestly, Jake, it just happened. The tickets were all booked in that name, and I'd had my passport altered in advance... And I didn't actually say anything. It just got assumed, and it was too complicated to correct it.'

For some reason, it seemed important to make him believe her—and not just because then he might leave her alone. 'Jake, when I thought you were Simon—I was horrified, not pleased. I suddenly realised that I didn't want to go back... I know you weren't exactly disinterested in what you did, but you were right about me. I was wrong to be marrying him, even if...if we hadn't happened.'

There was another silence. A somehow *dangerous* silence. And when he spoke again, Jake's voice purred with threat. ' "Not exactly disinterested..."'? What's that supposed to mean?'

His evasiveness when she was trying to be honest made her anger boil again. 'Oh, don't try and kid me, Jake. I know perfectly well that the real reason you didn't want me to marry Simon was to stop him getting his hands on Grandfather's inheritance. I suppose I should be grateful that you didn't decide to marry me yourself. Just to make sure.'

'I see.' The smouldering fury in his voice was so intense that Amber half expected the door between them to burst into flame. 'So that was why you decided to let me sweat it out there in that damned wood while you prepared yourself for marriage to the blue-eyed boy of the piece. Well, you needn't worry, Tiger-eyes. I can assure you that I have no intention of ever marrying again. And, even if I did, I wouldn't choose a little fool who could even contemplate tying herself up for life to a stuffed shirt like our mutual cousin.'

He paused and took a deep breath. 'What the hell do you think he wanted you for, Amber? Or did it escape your notice that old Matthew's will set him the same conditions it gave me?'

'That had nothing to do with it. Simon and I grew up together. We've always known——'

'Have you? That's not the way I remember it. Last time I saw much of the Farrells, it wasn't you that Simon was mooning after. It was your harpy friend with the nails. As I recall, you were left with your "uncle" Jake. But still——' he spoke with deliberate cruelty '—no doubt he was in a hurry. And you were...handy.'

Amber fought back the angry tears before she replied. 'That's not true! Why do you have to bring everything down to your own sordid level? Simon and I—we—he——'

'He what? Loved you? Oh, no—I forgot. You're not looking for anything as violent as *love*, are you, Amber? Just a "civilised partnership". And I've no doubt that my cousin found the idea of marrying you attractive enough, even without the sweetener of inheriting old Matthew's pile. All I'm saying is that his motives may have been mixed.'

His voice changed, and even through the thickness of the door between them, Amber thought she could feel his pain. 'Just as mine were, when I married, Tiger-eyes. I thought I could handle it. But I was wrong—and I won't let that happen to you. For old times' sake.' He raised his voice again, as if regretting his show of gentler emotion. 'Now will you come out of that bathroom? I'm beginning to feel like a prize idiot, conversing with a door.'

'Just let me take a shower, Jake.' She took his silence as consent and stepped into the cubicle at last, turning on a jet of water to drown out anything more he might say. She had plenty to think about already.

The water was cool and refreshing, subduing the flush of her skin to a rosy glow. But the thoughts kept spinning round inside her head. And even the coldest water couldn't quiet them.

At least Jake didn't try to pretend that Aunt Bella had been lying. Amber's long experience of her aunt's unbending rectitude made her certain that that was out of the question. That Jake had already made one unprincipled attempt at gaining his grandfather's inheritance was past dispute. But was it possible that, in her case, Jake's motives had been less self-interested than the older woman had believed?

After all, it had been chance, their meeting . . . He could never have planned to find her there, in the glade. And if his objective had really been to prevent her marriage, why had he left it so late to interfere? Surely he must have known about the engagement before?

But she had only questions, and the answers were locked inside Jake Farrell's brain. And there, no doubt, they would remain.

Ten minutes later, showered and swathed decently in one of the hotel's mercifully large bathrobes, Amber slid back the bolt and peered tentatively out into the room. There was no sign of Jake. And, to her surprise, the bed was already remade.

Such prompt action was such a contrast to the well-meaning and rather likeable inefficiency that the Balinese staff normally displayed that she felt a flicker of resentment against her unwanted visitor. Did Jake Farrell's methods always get him everything he wanted? If so, it was about time he was taught differently.

But realistically she knew that she was in no immediate position to teach him that very tempting lesson. If there was one thing the last few hours had taught her, it was that, in a clash with Jake Farrell, she could only lose. Her own body would betray her.

The only way out was to meet him halfway; to convince him that she was no longer in danger of marrying his cousin. Then, whatever his real motives were, he might leave her alone.

The prospect should have pleased her. But instead, she felt her eyes prickle, and a tightness at the back of her throat as she remembered the low thrum of his voice. 'A honeymoon is a game for two players.'

If this had been a real honeymoon... Amber shut off that train of thought with a mental snap. Although not before she realised that the man in the picture that rose involuntarily before her eyes was not Simon Farrell. But Jake. The vision of him as she had first seen him, naked and angry, returned to haunt her. And not just the vision. The very feel of him; the warmth of his body pressing against her; his hand on her mouth...

'Damn him,' she muttered fiercely to herself. 'I will not let him get to me.' And she hitched the bathrobe a little tighter around her waist, as if girding herself for battle.

But, as it turned out, the precaution was unnecessary. The calm that reigned over the cottage was soon explained when she went through into the sitting-room and found him stretched out on the sofa, innocently asleep.

He looked so peaceful that, just for a minute, she was reluctant to wake him. But a glance out of the window at the rapid darkening of the tropical sky convinced her. If she wasn't going to spend a night under the same roof as Jake Farrell, she would have to act quickly.

'Wake up, Jake.'

He yawned widely, then grinned. 'Well, at least this time you got my name right.' He sounded almost friendly. 'But don't I get a "darling"?'

Amber felt herself blush. 'No, you don't,' she retorted sharply, to cover her embarrassment. 'Look, Jake—you've reassured yourself that I'm all right, and that I'm not about to lure Simon out here and marry him by force, or whatever it was you were worried about. So what are you planning to do? You can't really stay here—you must see that.'

He looked up with an air of enquiring innocence. 'Must I? I don't see why. If you don't intend to offer me the hospitality of your bed, then this sofa seems to pull out into a perfectly adequate substitute.' A mocking smile creased his face. 'You don't have to worry, Tiger-eyes. You're an attractive girl, but you're not so irresistible that I can't be trusted under the same roof. And Bali has plenty of other compensations for the lonely male . . .'

Amber flushed red with embarrassment. 'But surely you'll want to be getting back to England——?'

Her heart sank as he shook his head. 'It's about time I took a holiday—and Bali is one of my favourite haunts. I thought I could hire a car and show you the island. Starting with this evening. I know an intimate little restaurant in Kuta—just right for honeymooners like us.'

He really was infuriatingly stubborn. 'I don't think that would be a good idea, Jake. Besides, I've already got a driver.' But, even as she said it, she realised that once again it was Jake who held all the cards. 'Oh... I suppose Ketut works for you, does he? I thought Simon had arranged it.' It was almost a relief to know that she didn't owe Simon that. Except that, if anything, it was worse to be in debt to Jake... She pulled her mind back. 'But I still don't think——'

'Then you should think—very carefully, Amber.' There was a touch of steel back in his voice, and Amber realised with a shiver that Jake was enjoying his power over her, like a predator toying with its prey. 'After all, this is our honeymoon—and if I'm to be denied the usual forms of honeymoon entertainment——'

'Which you most certainly are.' She could feel her face burning. 'And it isn't your honeymoon——'

'I thought we'd agreed that I've hijacked it?' He made it sound an ordinary procedure, like catching a bus. 'So you can hardly refuse to help me fill up the time. After all, if I get bored, there's no telling what—amusements—I might turn to.'

He glanced through at the double bed behind them, as if to underline his words. Amber felt a surge of panic. What really lay behind his decision to 'hijack' her honeymoon? He had had her almost convinced that Aunt Bella had been mistaken about his motives—but perhaps she was being naïve. And she still had the feeling that he

was playing a game of his own—and that it wasn't
Tigers in the Woods.

By letting him stay, she would be playing with
fire, and she knew it. He had already burned her,
after all. But for the moment Jake Farrell held
all the cards. And there was nothing she could
do but let him deal them out.

'So how did you find me here, anyway?' As she
nibbled another stick of *sâté* from the little clay
brazier on the table, Amber realised that she was
beginning to enjoy herself. The restaurant Jake
had brought her to was a revelation, with tables
tucked away between bushes and tiny streams in
an area that was half plant-decked interior, half
exotic garden.

But her own enjoyment of it disturbed her. It
would be all too easy to find herself drawn into
the romantic atmosphere of the place. And it was
important to remember that her role in Jake's
life was one of temporary irritant, not lover...

'What do you mean? It wasn't difficult—apart
from the fact that you were travelling under an
assumed name. And I know Bali pretty well.'

But she shook her head. 'No, I mean how did
you know I had decided to come to Bali after
all?' Jake's ability to storm into her life at the
most unexpected moments seemed so much part
of his character that it had only just occurred to
her to wonder. 'After all, I didn't know myself
until the morning the flight left. And Ketut was
here to meet me when I arrived.'

He looked at her assessingly. 'I'm not sure I
should reveal my contacts. You might put poison

in their tea. But I promise you that they had only your best interests at heart.'

'What, by sending you out here to bully me?'

He grinned a little shamefacedly. 'Well, no... I didn't mention that. I just said I wanted to arrange an escort; someone to look after you. You can hardly blame your mystery benefactor for that.'

'So why can't you tell me who it was?' In her mind, Amber started turning over the possibilities. Her aunt and uncle were the only people she had told, but she knew Marchings well enough to guess that the news would have spread rapidly. Mrs Atkins was bound to have told Sandra, and the taxi driver was a notorious gossip. But only one name seemed likely. 'Was it Sandra?'

If it was Sandra, then it would mean their friendship was intact... But Jake shook his head. 'My lips are sealed, I'm afraid.' He beckoned the waiter to order another two of the delicious iced strawberry cocktails that they were drinking. 'Let's change the subject, shall we?'

Amber stiffened. Here it comes, she thought. But to her surprise, he didn't try to talk about the wedding, or the events that had preceded it. Instead, he quizzed her about the university course she had followed, surprising her by his depth of knowledge about the subject of tourism, as well as his apparently genuine interest in her doings.

'You're very knowledgeable,' she said in curiosity. 'Are you still in the travel business? I thought Aunt Bella told me that you hadn't wanted to go into Farrell Travel.'

'Only because there was something else I wanted to do. Old Matthew understood—or at least I thought he did, though now it looks as if he'd always intended to try and lure me back into the family fold. But I always knew I wanted to run my own set-up. Person to Person is small by comparison, but we're beginning to make our mark.'

'Person to Person?' Amber was startled. 'But I've heard of them; of course I have. But I had no idea... You specialise in individualised holidays, don't you? You're getting a good reputation.' That was an understatement; the little company had been one of the travel success stories of recent years. With a shock, Amber realised that Jake Farrell must be well on his way to emulating his grandfather's achievement—and perhaps even his wealth. It made his claims of disinterest a great deal more feasible...

He seemed pleased at the compliment. 'I'm glad to hear it. That was what attracted me to the idea: the personal aspect. It really is the antithesis of a giant like Farrell Travel—that's one of the reasons I've always played down the family connection. I wanted to get back to the idea of helping people to do what they wanted to do— not making them choose like sheep from a few glossy brochures. The core of it is a whole network of people like Ketut; local people who really know the places my customers want to visit.'

'Well, if they're all like him, I can see why you're so successful. I feel as if I've seen more in this week than I would even have dreamt of on my own. It's a beautiful place. And the dancing!'

Jake smiled at her pleasure. 'So have you seen the Barong Dance yet?' He paused as the waiter arrived and set down two glasses of black, cloudy coffee on the table. 'That's one of the most spectacular.'

She nodded.

'What did you think?'

Amber sipped at the murky liquid a little tentatively before replying, but was pleasantly surprised to find it delicious, despite the sediment of undissolved coffee-grounds clearly visible in the base of her glass.

'It was a wonderful spectacle,' she said at last, choosing her words with care. 'But I'm not sure I really understood it. I thought the tiger-thing was supposed to be the "goodie" and the other one, with the fingernails and the bulging eyes and its tongue hanging out, was the "baddie", so to speak. Is that right?'

He smiled. 'That's right. Only the "tiger-thing" was the holy Barong and the other was the wicked witch Rangda. They're two of the main characters in Balinese mythology; you're bound to bump into them again.'

'That's what I thought. But then it didn't make sense... The Rangda got killed, or at least I thought she did. But at the end she came back and she seemed to be winning. And then it just seemed to stop. There wasn't a proper ending at all.'

'No fairy godmother appearing out of the wings, you mean, to banish the nasty characters forever and marry off the hero and heroine? No, I'm afraid Balinese drama isn't as simplistic as ours. It deals with the realities of life, not with pretence.'

She looked at him in amazement. 'What on earth do you mean? It was hardly realistic, Jake. Just the opposite, I would have thought.'

Jake dismissed this with a wave of his hand. 'Oh, of course the characters are fantastic. No, what I meant was that the Balinese don't feel the need for neat and tidy solutions as we do. You were puzzled by the dance because the ending seemed inconclusive and because it seemed to suggest that evil is never completely vanquished. But is that really so unrealistic? In terms of life, that is, not books and plays?'

'I suppose not.' The thought was oddly unsettling. 'But isn't that rather a depressing point of view? Surely it's better to believe that good will triumph in the end?'

'And then what? The end of the world?' Jake shook his head. 'No, the Balinese are the wisest people I know; and, whatever their religion is, it's not depressing. They know that the universe is a constant dance between opposing forces, and they are wise enough to celebrate that instead of fighting it.'

'What do you mean, celebrate it?'

'Well, for instance, every morning, the Balinese housewife will make an offering to the gods at her household shrine—and another, just as carefully made, will be placed on the ground by the door for the evil spirits. That way both are placated—and she can go about her business in the knowledge that she has done her bit to preserve the balance. And in the village temple, the Barong and Rangda masks are treated with equal reverence.'

She looked at him curiously. 'You sound almost as if you believe it.'

'I suppose I do. Good and evil are two sides of the same coin; and most people are a mixture of the two. The trick is to take both into account, and tread the balance between them.'

Amber shivered. 'It sounds... immoral.'

'Why? If a man does someone a good turn for a bad reason, the other person is still better off for it. So is that good or bad?'

His eyes caught hers as he posed the question, and Amber found herself held by the intensity of them. The question he asked seemed to have more than general significance. Was he referring to their own situation?

However mixed the motives that had inspired him to intervene in her wedding plans, could she really say that she was sorry? She realised now that she had been poised on the brink of the biggest mistake she might ever have made.

Or was her increasing trust of him an error of still greater magnitude?

Later that night, Amber lay in the air-conditioned darkness, listening to the night-noises of birds and lizards through the bungalow's thin walls.

She found it difficult to sleep. The evening she and Jake had spent together had confused and disturbed her more than she wanted to admit. Even to herself.

'Is that good or bad?' The question spun round and round inside her head as she battled for the sleep that wouldn't come. In the end, she had pulled her eyes away and given a joking answer.

But it hadn't been a joke. Afterwards, she had felt him looking at her and had had the strongest feeling that he had been testing her in some way, and that she had failed the test.

It seemed hotter than ever in the little bungalow. Had the air-conditioning failed? But the controls were in the other room, and with Jake sleeping there she didn't dare to creep through to investigate.

In sudden frustration, she sat up and pulled the constricting fabric of her nightdress over her head. It was damp, and the touch of it reminded her of the intimate warmth of the sheet that she had pulled back to reveal Jake's face, and the sharp warm smell of his sweat in the wide bamboo bed.

As she tossed and turned, Amber found herself wishing that she had slept on the sofa-bed and let Jake take the main room himself. Although she knew that the sheets had been changed, she could have sworn that his scent still lingered in their now damp and crumpled folds.

All the shameful memories she had so rigorously suppressed came flooding suddenly back, twisting her stomach with desire like a physical pain. How could she respond like this to a man she hardly knew?

And yet, a treacherous voice whispered inside her, she did know him. Had known him since that first kiss had awakened her womanhood, so many years before... With her body, she knew him. And now she knew the heights of ecstasy to which he could drive her...

With a groan she turned over and buried her face in the pillow, trying to expunge the memory of his body heavy on hers, and his flesh, urging. He was so close; so unbearably close. She had only to open the door; to go to his bed. Or not even that. With the sharpness of certainty, she knew that she had only to call his name and he would wake and come to her.

So vividly that it was almost a hallucination, Amber could visualise his mocking smile as he invited her into his arms; the soft strength of his lips as he kissed her; the warmth and maleness of his body as he enfolded her. She could feel again the soft wet caress of his tongue as he tasted the wine on her skin.

It was hours before she slipped into sleep at last. And even there, he followed her... She was watching the dancing again, in the torchlight at the hotel. On the makeshift stage in front of her, the devil dancers leapt and pranced.

But instead of the Rangda's bulging eyes and savage talons, her demons had lean, dark faces and eyes that flayed her with contempt. They had lips of fire and hands that tormented her with pleasure, leading her further and further down the pathways of desire, only to desert her at the last barrier——

And then she was climbing the hill to her thinking-place, although the trees were not the birch of her childhood, but slim-trunked palms. And in her nostrils there was the scent of incense, and in her ears the roar of the surf. But the grove was the same. And in the centre of it was a tall, dark figure. The man she had climbed the hill to find.

And as she ran towards him, Amber knew that it was going to be all right; that this time, it was really her lover... And her heart was bursting with happiness.

Until he turned, and his face was the face of a demon. And his eyes were coals of flame.

'Jake!' She woke, startled and sweating with terror, and for a moment it seemed only natural that he was there, standing over her, his saronged figure silhouetted against the early morning light. 'Jake——'

And then she snapped into wakefulness with a start of fear as she saw the hunger in his eyes and realised what he was looking at. Her tossing and turning had pushed the sheet to the floor beside her discarded nightdress and she was sprawled naked before him.

The way he was looking at her sent an electric jolt of fear and longing up her spine. But he didn't move as she scrabbled to the far side of the bed and grabbed the sheet to swathe it round her.

It only needed a spark to start a conflagration that would engulf both of them. 'Jake... Jake, you promised——'

He was still staring at her like a man entranced. 'You called me, Tiger-eyes. I only came through because I heard my name.'

'I was dreaming, Jake. Please...' She backed off slowly towards the bathroom. But her movement seemed to break the spell, and she saw his face twist with sardonic amusement. 'Oh, for God's sake, don't let's go through that again. I told you: you're safe—if that's what you want. Although I would say that erotic little exhibition casts a few doubts on whether that's true...'

'No! I don't need——'

But his voice cut in on hers, harshly. 'You don't know what you need, Tiger-eyes.' His eyes caught hers, and held them.

'But you might, if you listened to your dreams.'

CHAPTER SEVEN

AMBER'S cheeks were still burning with embarrassment and anger at her self-betrayal as, after scrabbling hastily into her clothes, she followed Jake down the path towards the hotel swimming-pool. She had to hurry to keep up and wished, not for the first time, that she had managed to master the Balinese women's easy grace of movement in her tightly wrapped sarong.

Jake was striding ahead with swimming trunks and shirt thrown casually over one shoulder. The *sarong pria* gave much greater freedom to the legs, but Amber was stubbornly determined not to ask him to slow down.

Despite her preoccupations, she couldn't help noticing the firm, muscular line of his hips and almost animal elegance of his gait in the kilted wraparound. She had rather despised the other male tourists she had seen trying to wear the native costume, around the hotel and outside. They looked self-conscious, foolish and usually markedly unattractive. The sarong's minimal covering painfully emphasised the slightest paunch or flabbiness, and its unconventionality to Western eyes required total confidence in the wearing.

But Jake's tanned skin was nearly as dark as the islanders', and his body was lean and hard. Despite his height, he wore the batik cotton as naturally as he might have worn a tailored suit or denim jeans.

Watching the muscles of his back move with the lazy rhythm of his strides, Amber felt a surge of quite inappropriate pride. As if he really were her husband, and this her honeymoon... She had to tear her eyes away, almost painfully aware of his physical presence. For her own peace of mind, she wished she didn't suspect that the sarong was his only garment.

When they arrived at the pool, it was completely deserted. Amber let her sarong fall to the ground and, by diving in at once and swimming the first length underwater, managed to avoid confirming her suspicions. By the time she surfaced again, Jake was decently clad in swimming-trunks and cleaving like a dolphin through the clear blue water.

For a while she clung to the ledge and watched him, admiring the controlled energy that propelled him up and down the pool. Then she lay on her back and let herself float, until her reverie was disturbed by what sounded like a small school of whales surfacing directly by her ear.

'Oh! Jake, what are you doing?' she demanded when she had splashed her way back to the edge and finished spluttering. But his answer took her by surprise.

'Apologising.' He reached out and touched her cheek, stroking a path through the water droplets that clung there. The gesture made her catch her breath, fearing her own reaction. But in fact the touch was oddly sexless, like that of a father caressing his child.

'I'm sorry, Amber,' he went on seriously. 'I came out here to Bali because I was concerned about you, about what I'd done to you—and all I've done so far is make things worse.'

'Concerned about me?' Amber could feel herself staring at him stupidly. This wasn't at all the line she had expected him to take—this almost avuncular tone. It scarcely fitted with what she had seen in his eyes on waking from her dream. And yet he sounded sincere...

'Yes, of course. I put you through hell in England, and since arriving here I've just piled on more pressure. We got off on the wrong foot yesterday, and this morning I've messed it up again. Though I do claim that I was subjected to more provocation than a man can reasonably be expected to withstand.'

He caught her eye, and Amber felt herself blush. 'But that's neither here nor there. I had no right to inflict my frustrations on you—nor to allow a perfectly ordinary case of sexual attraction to get in the way of what I came here to do. Which is look after you, Amber.'

'Look after me?' Why didn't she seem to be able to do anything except stupidly echo his words? 'A perfectly ordinary attraction...' She felt her jaw set slightly in annoyance. 'What do you mean, Jake? I don't need looking after.'

'I think you do. No one who has gone through what you have—what I've put you through— ought to be left alone. And I still feel a responsibility for you, my little cousin. That's why I made the original arrangement with Ketut—and that's why I decided in the end that I should really take care of things myself. I had some business in Jakarta last week, so all in all it worked out rather well.'

Jake smiled at her with such fatherly benevolence that she half expected him to pat her on the head. For some reason she didn't want to analyse, she felt more like hitting him on his.

'Well, I'm so grateful that you managed to fit me into your busy schedule,' she said waspishly. 'But really, it wasn't necessary. I was managing fine with Ketut's help.'

'But it's not the same as family, is it, Amber? You've suffered a shock—and you may need to talk about it. That's why I'm here.'

With a sudden movement that took her by surprise, Jake grasped the side of the pool and pulled himself out to sit, sleek and gleaming like polished wood, on the ledge above. Dark hair clung wetly to his chest and legs and Amber felt something twist painfully inside her.

But he was still speaking, in that calm, reasonable, utterly un-Jake-like tone that nearly made her explode with frustration. 'I'm here if you need me, little cousin. And don't worry—there won't be any more scenes like this morning. After all, you're hardly my type, and I don't suppose I'm yours. So we'll just stay friends—and enjoy our "honeymoon" together. I thought this afternoon I'd take you up to Ubud. How does that sound?'

'Oh, wonderful.' But if he heard the savage sarcasm with which she invested the word Jake gave no sign. And as he stood up and wandered off to fetch the towels, Amber plunged back

through the water in an effort to dispel the black
mood that had suddenly afflicted her.

She had been almost reconciled to this unstoppable man's hijacking her honeymoon. Their
dinner last night had shown that he could be a
fascinating companion when he wasn't actively
tormenting her, and there was no doubt that
sightseeing would be more fun with two.

'A honeymoon is a game for two players...'
There was some truth in that, although not in the
way Jake had meant it. She had no intention of
playing that kind of game, and she had planned
to make that perfectly clear.

So why did she find it so infuriating that Jake
Farrell had been the one to change the rules?

'What are those for, Jake? You can't be hungry
again already.' After a morning spent shopping
and looking round the art galleries of Ubud, they
had eaten lunch only a few minutes previously,
in a little restaurant overlooking a tree-lined
gorge. Amber was feeling distinctly bloated. That
black-rice pudding with coconut... But Jake had
been right, it had been too good to miss.

So now she watched curiously as her companion stowed two large packets of peanuts in
the small rucksack he carried slung over one
shoulder. Were they provisions for later? 'Are we
going to be walking far? Because, if so,
these shoes——'

'Don't worry, Tiger-eyes. It's not far. The
peanuts aren't for us; they're for some friends of
mine.' He dug further into the rucksack and
pulled out the two brightly coloured strips of

brocade that they had bargained for in the market earlier that morning.

'Here; we'd better put the temple sashes on now. This is holy ground, even outside the temple. And my friends are the guardians; I wouldn't like to upset them.'

Obediently, Amber wound the sash around the waist of her sarong, wondering as she did so what kind of friends Jake had, that they would be grateful for two bags of rather dusty-looking peanuts. And thinking at the same time that the wood they were walking through didn't look particularly holy, although it was refreshingly cool in the trees' dark green shade.

She felt a tug on her sarong and looked down, expecting to see one of the ubiquitous Balinese children who followed strangers everywhere, selling postcards or just amusing themselves at the foreigners' peculiar antics. But to her shock the fingers that gripped her, and the other hand held out in supplication, were wizened and wrinkled, like those of a tiny old man. And the face that peered shyly from behind the folds of her skirt was surrounded by grey fur...

'It's a monkey! Oh, Jake—isn't it tame!'

He shook his head. 'Not tame,' he cautioned. 'Don't try to handle them; they've got a nasty bite. But they know what they want; and they're used to their visitors supplying it.'

'Of course—the peanuts! Are these your friends?'

Jake grinned. 'Here, you'd better give him some, or he'll be getting impatient.' And reaching into the bag, he pulled out a few of the nuts and handed them over.

To Amber's delight, the monkey took her offering neatly and started to stuff it into its mouth. The wizened fingers felt oddly human on her hand.

There was a rustle in the trees, and two more monkeys arrived, holding up their hands like tiny beggars.

'Oh, quick—give me some more.'

'Just one at a time,' Jake warned. 'They'll take the whole bag if you give them a chance. And come on; let's keep moving, or we'll find ourselves surrounded.'

It wasn't an idle threat. As they moved further on into the forest, the scuttlings and scurryings around them multiplied, until Amber was fully occupied just keeping up with their demands. It was even a little frightening, as grey hands tugged imperiously at her clothing whenever she slackened in her largesse.

But the monkeys themselves were fascinating, like people in miniature, each with their own personality and place in the social structure of their tribe. Amber watched them, entranced, especially the mothers. These advanced more warily than their companions, with their babies clinging timidly to their fur and watching the proceedings gravely with their great round eyes.

Amber would have liked to touch one of the little ones, but it would have been impossible, even if Jake hadn't warned her against it with a shake of the head. Unlike the other monkeys, who grabbed for the peanuts with both paws open, the mothers kept one hand free to clasp protectively over their offspring whenever a human, or more aggressive monkey, was in range.

'I've almost finished these,' she said at last. 'Have you got any more nuts in there, Jake? There seem to be more arriving all the time.'

But Jake was staring distractedly up the path as if awaiting some new arrival. 'I have, but I don't want to use them up too soon. There's someone else I want you to meet first,' he said rather cryptically, then added almost immediately, 'Ah! Here he is.'

But, even if he hadn't spoken, Amber would have guessed that something was up. The chattering around them ceased almost instantly, and the clamouring hands fell away. One monkey after another dropped on to all fours and scampered away into the edge of the undergrowth.

It was like the scene in an old western, she thought fancifully, when the gunslinger rides into town and all the townsfolk take cover. Only where was the gunslinger . . .?

And then she saw him. Twice as tall as the animals they had already seen, the size and weight of a small child, but with an air of authority that could only have come from years of command, the old monkey moved with massive dignity down the path towards them.

His grey fur was tinged with white, especially round the face, giving him a look of venerability and solemn wisdom, like an Old Testament prophet. And he was very obviously and definitely male. Amber noticed that all the mothers hugged their babies closer as he approached, shushing them with worried little sounds.

As they watched, he sat down a few feet in front of them, with the air of a dignitary granting an audience, and treated himself to a long and indelicately intimate scratch.

Amber felt almost nervous, as if in the presence of royalty. 'Can I feed him, do you think?' she whispered to her companion. 'It seems a cheek, somehow—like offering the Queen a sandwich.'

Jake seemed to understand exactly what she meant. 'Think of it more as a tribute,' he suggested, pulling the last bag of peanuts from the rucksack and handing it over. 'Only don't——'

But it was too late. Amber had taken the bag and advanced the few paces towards where the patriarch sat, holding out in her right hand a selection of nuts. And, without blinking an eyelid or in any way disturbing his ponderous dignity, the great monkey had reached out to her left and snatched the whole bag from her grasp.

Only then did he return his attention to the few nuts she had actually been offering. As if they were almost beneath his notice, he crammed them into his mouth with a single sweep of his paw. And, having ascertained with a practised glance that there was no more to be had, he turned his back and lumbered carefully away, leaving his victim gazing open-eyed behind him.

'Well!' But before Amber could think what to say, a woman's laughter sounded like chiming bells behind them, and they both swung round to see a pretty Balinese girl coming down the path. She had a baby on her hip and a large basket balanced effortlessly on her head, and Amber noticed that she too was wearing a sash, as if visiting a temple.

'He is cunning, that grandfather. He does not like to wait and be polite.'

It was Jake who answered, with a little bow of greeting. '*Selamat sore, nyonya*. It is after all his right. He is the king here, and all these are his subjects.'

The woman smiled in agreement, and with pleasure at hearing the Indonesian greeting. 'Rajah and father and grandfather, all three. He is oldest monkey in the forest. But where are you come from, *tuan*?' She turned to Amber, including her in the conversation with a graceful flash of the eyes. 'And *nyonya*?'

'From England.' Amber struggled to remember the answer Ketut had taught her to this perennial question. '*Dari Ingerris.*'

The woman clapped her delight. 'Oh, very good! The *nyonya* speaks Bahasa also. But I must practise my English. Do you like the holy monkeys?'

'Oh, yes! Especially the mothers with their babies, like that one.' Amber gestured towards where one of the little ones was contentedly suckling. Most of the other monkeys had withdrawn.

'Oh, yes, they are pretty, the little ones. And you, *nyonya*? Do you and the *tuan* have children?'

Amber felt her face redden. She had become used to the locals' insatiable interest in the size and composition of her supposed family, but this was the first time she had been asked it in Jake's presence. 'Oh, no——' she started. But Jake broke in.

'Not yet,' he smiled. 'This is our honeymoon.' And Amber had to listen with increasing embarrassment to the woman's congratulations and her hopes for a long and fruitful union, before at last she smiled her apologies and continued on her way.

'What did you have to say that for?' she hissed at Jake when they were alone.

He looked at her in surprise. 'Why not? In Bali, there are only two answers to the question, "Do you have children?" "Yes" and "Not yet". A straight "No" would be very puzzling. And the only valid reason for it being "not yet" is that our marriage is only recent. Otherwise she would have felt sorry for you—and rather embarrassed. It would have been as if a casual acquaintance in England said "How are you?", and you started telling them how dreadful you felt. It might be truthful, but it isn't polite.'

But Amber still felt hot with annoyance at his lack of tact. 'Well, it was me who was embarrassed, Jake. You may be desperate to claim fatherhood, but——'

'What did you say?' His voice jerked her back like a rein, and Amber felt herself go cold. It had just slipped out . . .

'Nothing.' But her voice carried no conviction, even to her own ears. 'Honestly, Jake, I didn't mean anything. It was just something my aunt said...'

'About me? And Vicky?'

Presumably Vicky was—had been—his wife. 'Well, yes. But I don't—I didn't mean——'

'So tell me, then.' His face was shuttered and remote, but all the anger he suppressed there was distilled into the whip-crack of his voice. 'Just when did my darling aunt decide to favour you with these recollections?'

He paused and took a deep breath, but before Amber could decide on her answer he stormed on. 'No, don't answer that. It was after I phoned, wasn't it? I don't know what her version of events was, but I've no doubt it made me out to be somewhere between Bluebeard and the Marquis de Sade. I knew she would have done her best to poison your mind against me, but I had hoped she might refrain from dragging Vicky into it too.'

He broke off, as if inviting her to speak. But Amber said nothing. 'Well, go on, then! What did she say? Or are you going to condemn me without trial?' And, when she still hesitated, he flung down the rucksack in anger.

'Damn it, Amber—whatever that old harpy told you, don't you think I'm entitled to know? There are two sides to every story—even if neither of them is particularly pretty. I didn't come out of my marriage with any medals for good conduct, but the mistakes I made were honest ones. So tell me the worst. What did she say?'

Jake listened almost in silence as Amber stammered out her aunt's story. She had almost forgotten how damning it was. And when she reached the end, she waited anxiously for him to speak.

When he remained moodily silent, she prompted him gently, 'Jake—are you saying it isn't true? Perhaps I shouldn't have taken her word for it, but I've never known Aunt Bella to tell a deliberate untruth. And she seemed so sure...'

'Oh, it was true enough—as far as the facts went.' He had sat down on the muddy bank by the side of the path and was staring introspectively at his hands. 'But it wasn't like that... When old Matthew's will was read, she and Simon were so damn smug about the whole thing—so convinced that he would get the lot... I thought we should make some kind of deal, but they turned me down flat. I suppose they had reason to be confident. I'd never made any secret of the fact that I wasn't the marrying kind.' He looked up apologetically. 'And presumably Simon was already engaged to you.'

'Not officially.' Amber tried not to remember the haste with which he had made it official. No wonder Aunt Bella had been so unexpectedly co-operative... But to her surprise the realisation didn't hurt. Neither of them had been marrying for the right reasons, after all. 'But I suppose he would have known I would say yes.'

'That's what I thought. But their attitude really annoyed me. And, by sheer coincidence, Vicky had come to me for help just a few days earlier. We'd been friends at college—almost lovers once or twice, but somehow it never quite happened.'

Amber felt a quite irrepressible surge of jealousy, followed as quickly by shamefaced relief.

'Anyway, she'd been dumped by the man she was seeing and then she'd found out she was pregnant. So she came to me for help.'

'And you decided to marry her?' Amber couldn't quite keep the disapproval out of her voice. Somehow, the greed that seemed natural and forgivable in Simon fitted less well into the image she was forming of Jake. 'To get Grandfather's money?'

He shook his head violently. 'It wasn't like that. You have to see, Amber, that it really seemed more like a practical joke. I didn't want Farrell Travel—my own business was just beginning to take off then and I had no intention of abandoning it. But I did need some capital for expansion. Old Matthew had always led me to believe that I'd get a part-share in the business, and I'd planned to get Simon to buy me out ... But the way it was fixed up, I stood to get nothing. Unless I married and had a kid. And there was Vicky, desperate for a husband and surrogate father. Her family were very strict and she was afraid that they'd throw her out if they knew.'

He kicked moodily at a peanut shell that lay discarded in the dust. 'It seemed like the perfect solution. For—for various reasons, I had no intention of marrying otherwise. And this way I would inherit the business and take out what I regarded as my share of the capital. Simon could have had the rest—I only wanted what the old man had promised me. Then, if Vicky and I hadn't been able to stick being married to each other, we could have quietly divorced in a year or so's time and I'd have settled enough money on her to bring the kid up independently if she had to. We had it all worked out.'

'Only it didn't turn out like that.'

He shook his head, moodily tearing at a leaf from one of the overhanging branches. 'Vicky miscarried almost immediately after the wedding. It—it hit her hard, and I didn't know how to handle it. That's when I learnt that you can't play around with people's lives, Amber. If I'd been a real husband, I could have comforted her. As it was, she was on her own. And to make matters worse she got it into her head that she had lost the baby as some kind of judgement for marrying me for all the wrong reasons.'

'But that's ridiculous, Jake!'

'I knew that, but she wasn't in any state to listen to reason. She started drinking and was teetering on the edge of a complete breakdown. In the end, she convinced herself that the only thing that could save her was a divorce. I didn't want it to happen that way, but her psychiatrist told me that there was no chance of her improving until she could put the marriage behind her...'

He paused, and rubbed his hand across his eyes, as if reliving the pain. 'Your aunt told you I walked out on her... Well, so I did, if you mean that I walked out of the flat and left her in it. What else could I have done, thrown her out on the street? I went on paying the mortgage, but it had got so she couldn't bear the sight of me. So I went. But it's haunted me ever since.'

Amber wanted desperately to comfort him; to touch him. But he seemed more remote than ever. 'So what did you do then?' she asked tentatively. 'About the business, I mean?'

He shrugged. 'What I should have done in the first place, I suppose. I borrowed. It meant a hair-raising couple of years when one bad season could have bankrupted me outright, but we made it. And the rest, as they say, is history. There wasn't any alternative, which concentrated the mind. I knew that I'd lost any chance I'd ever had of Grandfather's money, and to be honest I was glad. If it had been offered to me on a plate I'd have turned it down. I think I saw it as some kind of penance.'

The memory of it seemed to feed his bitter-ness. 'And now, whether you believe me or not, I just don't need it. Simon can take the lot and good luck to him—I just didn't want him to get it by making the same mess of your life that I made of Vicky's. And that's the truth.'

The silence hung in the air between them. 'I'm sorry,' Amber said inadequately. 'I—I do believe you.' Then, summoning her courage, she went on, 'And Jake—I can see why the idea of my marrying Simon upset you so much. And you were right. I wouldn't have been happy in that sort of set-up. I wouldn't have made him happy. So perhaps it wasn't all wasted, what you went through...'

He looked up at her as her voice trailed away, and just for a second she saw a flash of deep emotion in his dark eyes. 'Thank you, Tiger-eyes. That means a lot to me.'

He reached out and ruffled her hair. And as they walked back in companionable silence Amber had the nagging feeling that something important had happened.

But she didn't know what it was.

CHAPTER EIGHT

Two weeks later, Amber still hadn't quite worked out what that moment of closeness had meant. Somehow, despite the time they had spent in each other's company, it had never been repeated. But what she did know was that it was a bright, sunny morning. And that there were only seven days of her 'honeymoon' left. And that she was wishing that it could go on for ever...

Jake was sitting opposite her at the breakfast table, his brow creased as he read the letter he had just collected from Reception.

'Who's that from, Jake? Business?'

'What? Oh, no.' He looked up at her with a rather preoccupied air and shook his head.

But Amber refused to let her companion's abstraction dampen her spirits. She took another spoonful of the savoury rice porridge which had become her favourite breakfast dish, and waved it in Jake's direction. 'I'm glad to hear it. I hope your staff know better than to disturb you on your honeymoon.'

But if he heard the joke he didn't react to it. And a passing waiter, apparently believing that her gesture was some new kind of summons, paused by the table.

'Yes, Mrs Farrell? Would you like something else?'

Amber shook her head and smiled, and the waiter moved away, leaving her thinking how odd everything was. After a couple of weeks, she was happily sharing her breakfast with a man she had previously thought of as her deadliest enemy. And it now scarcely disturbed her to be addressed as his wife.

In the time they had spent together, Jake Farrell had become part of her life; as if, in some way, they really were married. And yet, despite their growing ease together, she knew that she was further away than ever from knowing what made him tick.

Amber looked across at her 'husband', still frowning in concentration over the letter. Why was he still in Bali? Was he really just concerned for her? Or was there something more?

She sighed, wondering for a moment if she was being naïve. There was the obvious reason, of course: that he was still somehow pursuing Grandfather Matthew's inheritance. Looked at from the outside, it was the only probable explanation.

Except that surely by now he must be convinced that she had no plans for a reconciliation with Simon. Amber realised with a sense of shame that she had hardly given a thought to her ex-fiancé since Jake Farrell had walked back into her life and hijacked her honeymoon. Simon, Aunt Bella, the wedding—all that seemed like another world.

But if it wasn't that it was difficult to see what Jake hoped to gain by his continued presence—unless he had a more personal interest. Unless he wanted her himself... The thought came from nowhere, and Amber felt herself flush. Not that it was the first time the notion had crossed her mind, but always, before, she had forced herself to ignore it. It was just wishful thinking, after all; a natural consequence of the romantic setting and her physical response to Jake's undeniably male attraction.

And Jake himself, after that first day, had made it quite plain that he wasn't interested. True to his promise, there had been no more 'close encounters'—nor had he shown any signs of missing them. In fact he seemed to be pursuing one of the Balinese girls who patrolled the beach, selling sarongs and bikinis to tourists. Much of the time while Amber was swimming and sunbathing he spent sitting with the girl, talking and laughing...

Suddenly the porridge seemed less tasty, and Amber pushed it away. It wasn't that she was jealous, she told herself. But she couldn't help feeling the eyes of the other guests on them, seeing them as a honeymoon couple and pitying her for having a husband who was already beginning to stray. It was ironic, when he had stuck so rigidly to their 'hands off' agreement. More rigidly, indeed, than she had ever foreseen...

If she was honest, she knew there had been many moments, watching a sunset, or dancing together in the hotel's open-air disco, when she had wanted desperately for him to break his promises. To make just a movement towards her... But, every time, her signals had been resolutely ignored.

And although, in retrospect, she had schooled herself to be grateful to Jake for not further complicating the situation, she couldn't help wishing sometimes that he had forced her hand.

But he never had. And now there was only one week left.

She looked across the table to where Jake sat. The letter lay tucked back into its envelope by his plate, and now his dark head was bent over a map of the island, his fingers playing idly with a strand of wavy hair. He looked up, as if the intensity of her gaze had drawn him. And their eyes met.

And at that moment, like a fog lifting, it all became clear. The landscape of her own mind was spread out in the sunlight before her. And Amber knew that what she feared most had happened.

She knew what it was that she felt for him, this man who sat opposite her at the breakfast table. This man who wasn't her husband. Not wishful thinking; not any temporary passion; but something final and irrevocable.

It had come creeping in through the back door of everyday life while she stood on guard against it at the front. And now she could no longer deny it.

She had fallen in love.

'I told you that you'd feel sick if you had a second bowl of that porridge, Tiger-eyes. You'd better be careful—we're in for a bumpy ride this afternoon. I was going to tell you; Ketut left a message to say that there's a temple festival starting tonight at his village, and he's invited us to go along as his guests. But it's a bit remote and the roads aren't the best in Bali. Remember what happened yesterday—you only just made it out of the car.'

Somehow, Amber managed to gather her wits and sound suitably delighted at the prospect. As a restorative, Jake's down-to-earth comment was roughly as effective as a bucket of cold water, and about as unpleasant. But at least he hadn't guessed the real reason for her temporary coma.

If it hadn't been so painful, Amber knew that she might have been amused by the irony of the situation. Just as Jake had learned to ignore the attraction between them, she had fallen for it headlong. Only, to him, it was just an extra bowl of porridge...

It was a relief to follow his change of subject, silencing the questions that clamoured for answer inside her head. 'Oh, Jake, that sounds marvellous. And how kind of Ketut to invite us!' Every temple in Bali had an *odalan* festival to mark the anniversary of its founding, and the colourful ceremonies were a frequent spectacle on the island. But to attend one as a guest was an unexpected treat.

'I'll wear my new blouse; the silk one. And the earrings I bought in Celuk.' Amber's voice chattered on, as if by talking she could drown out her new knowledge. 'And I'm sure I won't be sick. I don't know what happened yesterday—it must have been setting off straight after breakfast that did it. After all, I've eaten two bowls of porridge almost every morning since I arrived.'

Jake raised his eyebrows. 'There's no need to boast about it, you little glutton. How you keep your figure, I really don't know.'

She was conscious of a ridiculous pleasure that he had noticed her figure at all. But it was dampened almost immediately, when Jake stood up and waved to a pair of women approaching from outside the hotel.

At first they were just figures, one young, one old. But as they drew nearer the young one at least became only too recognisable.

She was dressed in her best sarong and her long black hair was garlanded with white flowers. But it was the girl from the beach. And Jake was quite obviously expecting her.

'*Selamat pagi, ibu, nona.*' Although it was to her that Jake addressed himself, the younger woman only giggled and left it to her companion to reply to his greeting.

'*Selamat pagi, tuan.*' The old woman's face crumpled into a smile, exposing a mouth and teeth stained red as if by blood. Amber shuddered, although she knew the horrific effect was only the result of chewing betel nut—a habit with many older Balinese.

Jake spoke rapidly for a few minutes in Indonesian, while Amber half listened and tried not to notice the undoubted beauty of their younger visitor. Her fragile looks were more those of a girl than a woman, and yet she had a woman's ripe figure and dark, exotic eyes. On her head, with the effortless grace that Amber never ceased to envy, she carried a basket and rolled-up straw mat. Perhaps she was selling something?

But just what was Jake telling them? Amber heard her own name mentioned, and the two women turned to look at her and laughed. She forced, with difficulty, a smile. And then Jake turned back to her.

'Amber, I'm forgetting my manners. This is Wayan, whom you'll remember from the beach. And this is her grandmother. I've asked them to do us a favour.'

'Oh——' What kind of favour could this oddly matched pair possibly do? she wondered. *'Terima kasih,'* she said carefully. 'Thank you.'

Jake seemed to be enjoying himself tremendously. 'These ladies are two of Bali's greatest artists,' he expanded. 'In the art of massage...'

'What?' Amber felt herself thrown completely off balance. Surely he couldn't mean...? She had heard, of course, of the sort of things that went on in some Eastern cities, but here...

Her confusion must have shown clearly on her face. Jake laughed. 'Don't look so startled, Tiger-eyes. Their intentions are entirely honourable, I assure you. A Balinese massage is something not to be missed. It will relax you so much that you'll hardly miss the sleep you lose tonight at the *odalan.'*

Amber opened her mouth to demur, but then realised that refusal was going to be impossible without hurting the women's feelings. So instead she smiled weakly and followed as Jake led the way back to the bungalow, planning all the things she would say to him when they were gone.

Once inside, Jake pushed the sofa back against the wall and the girl spread her mat in the centre of the floor.

'The trouble with European beds,' Jake explained, 'is that they are fine for sleeping on but hopeless for massage. Far too soft, and the wrong height. Sand is better—Wayan and her grandmother normally cater to tourists on the beach, but I thought you might prefer a little privacy.'

'You presumed right,' Amber said grimly. But she could see that her annoyance only amused him. 'Well, you can go first.'

'Very Eastern of you.' He untied his sarong and lay face down on the mat with his head cradled on his arms. 'Oh, by the way,' he added, his face hidden and a note of triumph in his voice, 'I suggested my wife might like a lesson...'

'What?' But before she could protest Amber found herself being pulled round into position by Jake's right shoulder. The old woman was opposite her and the girl was by her side. Giggling shyly, the girl took her unwilling hand and poured into it some warm oil from a bottle in her basket. It felt thick and silky on her skin.

Then she poured some into her own and started to spread it evenly over Jake's back with light, strong strokes. The fragrance of it seemed to fill the room, evoking for Amber all the scents of Bali. Coconut; sweet tropical flowers; a hint of spice... Its sweetness seemed to go to her head like wine. And then the old woman took hold of her hands and guided them into position. And the lesson began.

At first, Amber had to steel herself to touch the glistening flesh, fearing that the touch of it would only serve to reawaken the feelings she had so carefully buried. But to her surprise, that didn't happen. Instead she became more and more engrossed in the patterns her fingers were weaving across Jake's silky oiled skin.

The old woman demonstrated and Amber copied her, matching her motions to those of Wayan by her side. It no longer mattered that she didn't speak their language. Their hands spoke to her.

They told her of the muscles in Jake's back and chest, and she traced them with her fingertips, feeling the tension melt from them as they worked. They spoke of the breadth of his shoulders and the length of his thigh. Until his body was no longer something to be feared, but a canvas for their artistry. And Amber forgot all her embarrassment in the fascination of this new skill.

Not until the old woman sat back on her heels and indicated that the massage was over did Amber realise how tiring it had been. Her arms, particularly her left arm, felt like jelly.

So when Jake stretched and stood up to reach for his sarong, towering like a giant over the kneeling women, she was content to take her place on the mat. To her relief—or disappointment; she wasn't sure which—it didn't seem that he was planning to take an active part in her massage. Wayan gestured that she should take off her watch, and as she did so, she noticed the time. Her respect for the women grew. Jake's massage had lasted almost an hour and now they were starting again . . .

She felt their strong fingers spreading the fragrant oil over her skin. And with a sigh of contentment, she abandoned herself to the experience.

It seemed like an eternity later when they turned her over to lie on her back. She could see Jake lying back on the sofa, his eyes half closed. And then the old woman laughed and said something to him in her own language.

The effect was startling. Jake's face went pale under his tan, and he jerked back to wakefulness with a start. He fired off a volley of Indonesian; questioning, Amber thought, from the tone of his voice. Or demanding.

The old woman replied calmly, never for a moment interrupting the gentle rhythm of her fingers on Amber's stomach.

Jake stood up abruptly. 'I'm sorry, Amber. I've just remembered something. I'll pick you up here after lunch.' He walked out of her line of sight into the bedroom, and she could hear him dressing. And then the door slammed and he was gone.

Oh, well, she would ask him later. It could hardly be important . . . And with a mental shrug of the shoulders, Amber slipped back into a languorous, fragrant dream.

But by one o'clock Jake still hadn't returned and even Ketut, with his Balinese indifference to the niceties of time-keeping, had started to murmur his concern.

'Perhaps it will be better if I return to my village?' he suggested tentatively. 'And Tuan Farrell can drive you when he returns.'

Amber looked at her watch, even though she knew perfectly well that it couldn't be more than five minutes since she last consulted it. 'Well, I suppose you could... Only you know Mr Farrell said he wasn't sure of the route. Oh, dear.' She looked back at her watch. 'I'm sure he'll be back soon... But if only I knew where he'd gone.'

'Perhaps he is call away on business? Important communication, perhaps? Tuan Farrell have much business in Indonesia.'

'Does hc? I suppose he does.' Amber felt obscurely cheated that the little Balinese should know so much more about her supposed 'husband' than she did herself. But his words jogged her memory. Important communication... 'Oh—of course! It must have been that letter.' Quickly, she explained about the letter Jake had received at breakfast. 'And he did look rather worried—but if that was it why didn't he do something about it then? And I'm sure it was something that old woman said.'

But Ketut shook his head. 'I do not think that is a likely thing, *nyonya*. What could an old massage-woman say about business? I think Tuan Farrell remember something that he must do because of letter.'

'I suppose you're right. Look, Ketut, what's the latest you can leave?'

He shrugged, as all the Balinese seemed to when an attempt was made to tie them down to times. 'Perhaps two, perhaps three o'clock. You understand, there is much to do in village. And my wife——'

'Oh, we mustn't make you late!' She made a sudden decision. 'Look, why don't you wait here in Reception, Ketut? And I'll go back to the bungalow in case Jake's left me a note. Then, if he hasn't appeared by two o'clock, you'd better go on. But I'm sure he will be here.'

She sounded more sure than she felt. But as she hurried back towards the cottage she was trying to visualise exactly what she and Jake had done when they had returned from breakfast with the two women. She could see him walking in, and dropping the map casually on to the table by the window. Just the map? Or had there been something else...?

'But I'm sure he didn't take it with him,' she muttered to herself. And if the mysterious letter was still there it might tell her something. Amber felt herself flush a little in embarrassment at the thought of reading Jake's correspondence. But, for some reason she couldn't quite fathom, that was exactly what she intended to do.

...don't know how you picked it up, but it looks as if you may be right about my son and his childhood sweetheart. Of course, he is still outwardly heartbroken, but I can't help feeling that it's mainly because he enjoys young Sandra's very able comforting... Perhaps I'm an old cynic, but I wouldn't be surprised if there was a wedding in the family soon, after all.

Well, if there is, then good luck to them,

and my dear wife will just have to grit her teeth and put up with it. I blame myself very much for not taking more care to make sure that Simon and Amber really cared for each other and were not merely being swept along by the force of Bella's determination. She means well, but she is far too inclined to see things as she wishes them to be, regardless of reality.

So thank you for the hint, and for the reassurance about the old devil's money. You really are being extraordinarily generous about this, Jake—and, as you say, if things do work out like that, and Simon inherits the precious business, it will be a great deal easier to talk Bella out of her 'never darken my doorstep again' act as far as Amber is concerned. I think she's weakening—she really is quite fond of the girl, despite all her bluster.

I'll leave it to you to decide how much of this to pass on to Amber. Look after her for me. I'm very grateful to you for taking the trouble to fly out personally to take care of things.

The letter was signed, 'Bob Farrell'. Amber stared blankly at its pages, trying to take in what she had learnt. So it had been Uncle Bob who had given away her whereabouts to Jake. Somehow that had never occurred to her, although, now she knew, it did make perfect sense. Perfect sense, that was, to anyone who trusted Jake...

And her uncle plainly did trust him... From the sound of it, Jake must have told him the full story, including the reasons why he no longer had any designs on old Matthew's coffers. No wonder he was congratulating Jake on his generosity.

She should have been delighted to have her own instincts about Jake confirmed, but instead Amber was conscious of a mounting sense of panic. Why hadn't Jake told her about her uncle's letter? He must have known that she would be eager for news. And yet he had sat opposite her at breakfast and read it and not said a word.

And now he had disappeared... That was the real reason for her panic. Ketut was right; it was much more likely that his sudden departure was to do with the letter he had received than that he had rushed off as a result of anything the old woman could have told him. But if the secret was in the letter what was it? And why wasn't he back?

A terrible suspicion was forming like a dark cloud in her thinking. She turned back to the letter. 'I wouldn't be surprised if there was a wedding in the family soon, after all...'

The questions buzzed round in her head. What if she had been wrong about Jake, after all? What if Jake Farrell had deceived both her and her uncle, and was really just using her—when all he was really interested in was Grandfather Matthew's inheritance?

What if he had realised from the letter that all his plans were about to be ruined?

And what if he didn't come back?

CHAPTER NINE

'OH, JAKE!' Amber almost threw herself at him as he came through the door. 'I'm so glad you're back! Where were you? I've been so worried.'

He looked a little taken aback. 'Well, it's nice to know you miss me, Tiger-eyes,' he said, ruffling her hair. 'I didn't mean to be so long. But what's got you so excited? Has anything happened?'

'Oh, no.' Amber looked surreptitiously behind her at where the letter lay, now safely returned to its envelope as if it had never been touched.

She felt rather foolish. You could hardly say, 'I was worried because I'd been reading your private correspondence and I thought you might have nipped off back to England to break up a few more marriages.' In fact, the more she thought about it, the more ridiculous the whole idea seemed.

'I was just worried we would miss the *odalan*,' she came up with at last. 'Ketut wants to leave as soon as possible, otherwise I gather his wife will be cross with him. And as I didn't know where you'd gone... What was it, Jake? Was it something that old woman said?'

But Jake proved oddly evasive about the reason for his hurried departure. 'What? How could it be? I've never met the old crone before; she only came along to chaperon her granddaughter. You were half asleep, Tiger-eyes; you must have got it muddled. Now, let's get moving, shall we? I was thinking we could go via Penelokan and give you a look at the volcano on the way.'

For some reason, Amber was almost sure that he wasn't telling the truth, but although it was intriguing it didn't seem worth risking an argument. And as she followed him out to meet Ketut she was conscious of a disagreeable sense of flatness. It wasn't that she wasn't delighted to find that her dire suspicions were unfulfilled. It was just that, somehow, the implications of the letter had depressed her.

Although it was comforting to know that her uncle, at least, was still on her side, it did leave her wondering just what Jake's role really was. There was that last line, where her uncle thanked him for coming out...

If it had been her uncle's idea that Jake should come out to Bali and look after her, as a sort of avuncular stand-in, then it solved the main mystery of why he was here.

But Amber realised from her disappointment that she had been secretly hoping that there was quite another reason...

But the excitement of the forthcoming festival put her worries temporarily out of her head. It was the first time she had travelled with Jake in Ketut's *bemo*. Their other trips together had been by hired car. And she soon decided that Jake as a fellow passenger was very different from Jake as a driver.

For a start, he seemed far more relaxed—not surprising in view of the terrifying way the islanders drove. He had lost the feeling of distance that she had noticed on their other trips, talking freely and amusingly about the people and places they were passing. In fact, he was becoming almost attentive...

The lurchings of the little truck threw her heavily against Jake's side. He didn't draw away, and his arm, which had lain along the back of the seat, curled gently round her shoulders.

Amber felt a glow of contentment spreading through her. It was as if he had read her mind and set out to comfort her. But she was determined not to read too much into what might be just a friendly gesture.

She sat there, hardly daring to breathe. The damp warmth of his body pressed against her through his shirt, stirred by the gentle motion of his breathing. And when she turned to look up at him he smiled, the corners of his eyes crinkling with what might have been affection. It turned her heart to jelly...

It was such a small start, but at least it was a beginning. Like the first drip forming on the tip of an icicle, it might mean nothing in itself. But it carried the promise of spring.

They were driving now through bamboo forests, and it was impossible to see beyond their immediate surroundings. But the road sloped upwards ever more steeply, and the air was noticeably cooling. Amber wrapped a second sarong around her shoulders, glad that Jake had warned her what to expect. 'Is this the side of the volcano?' she ventured.

Jake shook his head. 'Not exactly; not of Mount Batur itself. The place we're heading for is called Penelokan, which means "Place for Looking". You'll see why when we get there.'

And she did. A few minutes later, the forest cleared and the truck drew to a halt by a stall at the side of the road. Amber followed Jake out, not quite knowing what to expect. But the view that greeted them took her breath away.

They were standing on the rim of a vast extinct volcano, the valley before them stretching into the misted distance like a country from a dream. And on the far side of that ancient crater, and almost dwarfed by it, rose another mountain, a trail of smoke leading from its summit. Mount Batur; a mountain within a mountain. And at its roots, like a sheet of silvered glass, there lay a lake.

'Oh, Jake... It's beautiful. It almost hurts to look.' There was something about the colours, muted and yet glowing, as if the air through which they were filtered was made of finer, more delicate stuff.

'The "Navel of the World", someone has called it.' For a moment, Jake's voice was husky with emotion. 'That's how I've always thought of it. The world in its innocence; unspoilt; untouched by man.' He shook his head, and when he spoke again his voice was normal. 'Not that it's true, of course. Not even here. But the illusion is magical.'

And, looking down into the crater, Amber could feel his closeness. And the magic seemed very real.

'Oh, my goodness.' The groan was shaken out of her. 'Are we nearly there?' Amber had travelled some difficult roads since her arrival in Bali. Potholes seemed to be the norm, rather than the exception, and the occasional attempts made at repair by filling them with rocks only made matters worse.

But the track down to Ketut's village made the rest seem like models of highway engineering. Even the sturdy little *bemo* was reduced to travelling at a snail's pace and, despite Jake's amused reassurance, Amber began to wonder if they would ever arrive. But at last they passed through the stone gateway that marked the limits of the village and a few minutes later were driving up the main street.

It was obvious at once that something unusual was happening. On both sides of the roadway, young women and girls were setting up food stalls and laying out their wares. And as they drove slowly past the temple, Amber saw that each of the lion-headed stone figures that guarded the entrance had been provided with a sarong of chequered cloth, a red silk parasol and a waxy white flower behind its ears. The whole place was alive with festive preparation.

As they climbed down from the *bemo*, Ketut introduced Amber proudly to two of his brothers, who bowed and smiled a welcome. Other villagers flocked round, and, instead of being a

tourist, Amber found herself and Jake treated as
honoured guests. But then a little girl of about
three emerged squealing from the compound to
drag her father inside, and Ketut led them away
in triumph to meet the rest of his relations,

As he showed them round his home, Amber
realised that Ketut must be a man of some importance in the village community. Inside a
walled courtyard, several thatched huts housed
kitchen, bathroom and sleeping quarters for the
numerous members of his family. Another, more
elaborate building with carved pillars turned out
to be his rice barn, decorated in honour of the
spirits of the rice. And in one corner was a small
family shrine, echoing in miniature the elaborate
architecture of the temples.

Like its larger counterpart in the village, this
too was dressed for the festival, and offerings of
fruit, rice and flowers were piled high before it.

His wife, Made, greeted them proudly in
broken English, then introduced her children.
There were four; two sons, the little girl,
Nyoman, whom Amber had already met, and a
baby—another daughter. Amber tentatively advanced her complimentary phrase, and was rewarded with a shy smile of delight.

'My wife does not speak English well,' apolo-
gised Ketut. 'But she is very happy to see you.
She will show you now your room. I hope you
will be comfortable in my house. It is small, not
like hotel.' He paused a moment in obvious pride
and said impressively, 'But I have a very fine bed.
It is English bed; very comfortable for foreign
people. Not like Balinese bed.'

An awful suspicion was beginning to form itself in Amber's mind. 'Jake——'

But her companion seemed determined not to hear her whispered protest and she found herself being ushered towards one of the smaller pavilions.

'Selamat datang.' Made opened the bamboo framed door and gestured them to enter. 'You are welcome. Bedroom here. And to bathe——' She pointed towards a hut at the back of the courtyard. 'Bathe is here.'

There were no windows in the wall of their 'bedroom' and it took Amber's eyes a few moments to adjust to the gloom. But when they did what she saw struck her dumb with panic. Almost the whole floor-space of the hut was taken up by a huge brass bedstead that would have looked more at home in a Victorian mansion. One bedstead. A double.

Behind her she could hear Jake thanking their hostess for her kindness, and Amber knew she ought to join in. But the power of speech seemed to have deserted her. She waited wordlessly until they were left alone.

When she finally spoke, her voice sounded strange to her own ears. 'Is this the only room they've got?' she hissed. 'We can't both sleep here.'

'I'm afraid we're going to have to. And keep your voice down; these walls are only woven mats. This bed is obviously Ketut's pride and joy—God knows where he got it from, but I would guess it's some kind of heirloom. If we turn it down, he'll be mortally insulted.'

She looked at Jake in despair. He was smiling, treating it all as a joke. And to him it might be. But to her... She clenched her fists. 'Then you'll just have to explain, Jake! It's all your fault for letting him think you were my husband...'

She broke off and looked wildly round for inspiration, but none was forthcoming. She couldn't—wouldn't share a bed with Jake. It would be the end of any hopes of concealment... If she had betrayed herself once in her dreams, it could happen again. And with him lying so close—with the touch of his body against her—how could she not dream?

Oh, why did this have to happen now, just when his attitude to her seemed to be softening? 'There must be something that you can say; some excuse you can give,' she went on desperately. 'They must have other rooms.'

But he shook his head. 'They don't go in much for privacy in Balinese families, Amber. Probably the only other bedroom is Ketut and Made's—everyone else will sleep out on that platform in the courtyard. Not that they'll be doing much sleeping tonight. But there is one other possibility.' Jake looked at her with an odd expression on his face. 'It depends how important this is to you. There is another way. Women don't sleep with their husbands during their monthly periods; there is a separate hut.'

Amber sighed with relief, ruthlessly suppressing the involuntary surge of disappointment that accompanied it. 'Then that's the answer. We just tell them——'

'Hear me out, Amber; it's not as simple as that. If you tell them that, you won't be allowed into the temple or anywhere near the offerings. In fact, I'll really have to take you home. Women at that time are considered *sebel*; unclean. It's one of their strictest prohibitions. Surely you must have seen the notices by the temples?'

'Oh.' Now that he mentioned it, Amber did remember seeing the notices. She had laughed at their quaint wording but, as they hadn't applied to her, had thought no more of it. A small frown creased her face. That memory had sparked off a thought—but it had slipped away before she could grasp and examine it.

Jake said gently, 'Would it be so terrible, Amber? It wouldn't be the first time that we've slept together, after all.' He had never before referred so directly to the night in the glade, and Amber looked up at him, alerted by something in the tone of his voice.

And then Jake was speaking again, but with an urgency and passion that she hadn't heard before. And this time, there was nothing of the 'uncle' in it. Only the man . . . 'Amber, I've tried to give you time,' he said huskily. 'But I can't wait forever. I love you, and I think you care for me.'

She just stared at him, unable to believe that she was really hearing the words she had longed for. It was as if the world had suddenly twisted on its axis, to show a completely different face. She had been all wrong . . . All wrong about everything. She had thought she understood him. But she had known nothing at all.

Jake reached out and cupped her chin in his hand, tilting her face so that she looked directly into his eyes. 'There's nothing to be afraid of, Tiger-eyes. If you want, we could sleep here tonight and I won't touch you. But that's not what I want. I want to make love to you, Amber. And you want me.'

The voice that answered seemed to well up from depths beyond her control. 'Yes...' But she had to be sure... Nothing made sense. What if she was wrong here as well? 'But Jake——'

'No buts, my love.' He bent slowly to brush his lips on hers and the touch started a fire smouldering inside her. 'What happened between us in that glade was more real than any marriage. You belong to me, Amber, and I won't let you go. Not ever again. When we get back to England, I'll marry you properly. If we get a registrar's licence, we could be married in a couple of days. But it will never be more real for us than it is tonight.'

Marry you... 'I don't understand.' But the words were simple enough. 'Oh, Jake—are you sure? You said you didn't want to marry again. You said——'

'I know what I said. But I was a fool. You weren't the only one to be afraid, Amber. But not any more.'

Without waiting for an answer, he drew her towards him, and his mouth sought hers. And then his lips were caressing her, first lightly and then with increasing passion. And he was crushing her body against him until she could hardly breathe.

'Oh, my darling, my precious darling.' He
buried his face in her hair and she could feel his
breath warm on her neck. 'It was torture to have
you so near and not be able to touch you . . . hold
you.' One hand slipped round under her blouse
to cup her breast, holding it like delicate por-
celain in his palm.

His thumb gently stirred the hardening tip and
Amber sighed with pleasure. His weight pressed
down on her. And she sank back slowly on to
the bed.

A sudden cacophony of shrieks and wheezes
from the ancient springs filled the air, and they
shot apart like children discovered in mischief.
Amber started to giggle helplessly.

'You realise what this means?' She panted out
the question between gasps of laughter. 'We can't
possibly——'

'Oh, no. If you think you're going to put me
off again, woman, you can think again. You
underestimate my versatile intelligence—and my
level of desperation.' Jake twisted his face into a
melodramatic leer. 'You may have escaped my
clutches now, pretty maiden, but come the dawn
you will be mine! All mine!' And he pulled her
towards him to claim her with his lips.

The return of Made a few minutes later, with her
baby on her hip, made Amber grateful for the
bed's timely interruption.

'She says, would you like to go with her and
the other women to help to prepare the offerings?' Jake translated. 'Then, later, she'll help
you dress.' When she hesitated, he pushed her

gently. 'Go along, Tiger-eyes. I'll see you later.'
His voice was full of meaning and the words sent
shivers of anticipation down her spine.

Reluctantly, she let herself be led away. But
soon she was feeling a happy empathy with the
graceful little woman despite their lack of
common language. Amber found herself wishing
that she could tell Made about Jake's proposal,
feeling that to put it in words and hear the other
woman's congratulations might have made it
seem more real. Everything was changing so
quickly... Her own memories of the scene in the
little hut now had the texture of a dream.

But even if they had been able to speak to each
other, Amber realised, it would still have been
impossible to confide. As far as Made was concerned, she and Jake were already married. So
perhaps it was as well that speech between them
was restricted. Where words would have been
awkwardly constrained, their language of smiles
and gestures could range freely. And Amber soon
found herself happily playing with the baby while
the other women worked.

Even the little girl, Nyoman, had her part to
play, carefully decorating the tall mounds of
coloured rice-cakes with flowers to form part of
the family's temple-offering. Ketut and the boys
had disappeared, and Made explained, with the
help of her few words of English, that they had
taken Jake to watch a cock-fight with the other
men of the village.

Amber could hear their excited shouting, but
felt no urge to go and look, preferring to watch

the intricate decoration of the food-offerings—
just as traditional and less brutal. And besides,
she knew that she would have felt out of place.
None of the other women showed any interest in
what was plainly a male preserve.

At last, when everything was ready, Made took
Amber into their hut to help her dress, showing
her how to arrange the broad sash and decorating her hair with flowers. Amber's fiery hair
especially seemed to fascinate her as she inter-
laced it with the plump, waxy petals, her fingers
weaving in and out with practised skill.

Suddenly, a thought seemed to occur to her.
'You do not have ...' She pointed shyly at
Amber's midriff, as if hunting for words. 'Time
of moon, for woman, you do not have now?'

Amber blushed as she hastened to reassure her
hostess, remembering how close she had come to
making just that excuse. And, again, she felt that
flicker of something at the back of her mind. The
ghost of a thought ... But it eluded her again.

And then the men returned from the cock-fight
and retired to wash and change. Jake emerged
resplendent in ceremonial sarong and head-dress,
to be complimented and giggled at by the women
of the household who flocked around him like
fragile humming-birds around a hawk. Amber
felt her heart swell tight with pride and knew,
from the moment of silence when he first saw her
on his return, that Made's work had had the same
effect on him.

But there was no opportunity for privacy. The
festival was gathering momentum and a carnival
atmosphere prevailed as more and more

worshippers arrived, the women carrying the towering offerings effortlessly on their heads.

Little Nyoman had been given the task of looking after their guests and took her responsibilities seriously. Amber and Jake were steered around temple and courtyards, their small keeper tugging busily at their sarongs if she considered her charges in danger of missing anything.

The whole ritual had a friendly simplicity unlike anything that Amber had expected. As each family arrived with their offerings, they joined the procession into the temple. There the women, even the oldest, joined in a stately offering dance as the beautiful arrangements of fruit and flowers were given to the gods. Each person was sprinkled with holy water and received a blessing, symbolised by a few grains of rice pressed against forehead and cheek.

The dusk was gathering now, and the air was heavy with the smell of flowers and incense and filled with the clamorous, bell-like music of a gamelan orchestra in the outer courtyard. The area around the temple was crowded, and people milled cheerfully around, eating snacks bought from the food-stalls and chatting and laughing with their neighbours.

But then, as if in response to some secret signal, the villagers started to gather round the edges of the courtyard where the gamelan played. Children appeared from nowhere and jostled for the best view and Nyoman hurried her charges into what she considered their proper place at the front. The air hummed with expectancy.

And then the dancing started. It was the Legong dance, the quintessential dance of Balinese femininity, and Jake whispered to her that this troupe of dancers was one of the island's most renowned. Amber had seen its graceful movements enacted the previous week at the hotel. But she realised that, although that had been a polished performance, this was the real thing.

The dancers, bound tightly in their splendid gilded costumes, were dancing on another plane, lifted out of the ordinary realms of human skill to something which was magical in its intensity.

Amber drank it in, as absorbed as the other members of the audience in the subtle language of music and gesture which somehow spoke directly to the heart. And when the chiming notes of the orchestra drew to a close and the dancers ran gracefully off into the tropical night, she felt as if she had been snatched back from fairyland.

But if the dancing was over, the celebrations had only just started. There was another long and chatty interlude before the crowd regrouped, this time around a white cloth screen stretched out as if for a makeshift cinema.

After the traditional beauty of the dancers, Amber felt obscurely disappointed by this apparent lapse into modernity. 'What happens now?' she whispered sleepily to Jake. 'Some kind of film?'

'Not exactly, sleepy-head. This is a shadow-puppet show. We'll watch it for a bit, then creep away.'

'Won't they mind? I wouldn't like to upset them.' But her head was feeling heavier and heavier as it leaned against his arm.

His voice was gentle. 'Don't worry, Tiger-eyes. It will go on now until dawn—and no one will notice if we leave. The Balinese seem to find these shows unfailingly fascinating, but I must admit that I always fall asleep after the first hour. And you look halfway there already.'

So for a few minutes she watched the intricate puppets strut and posture on the screen, until the wailing chant of the narrator seemed to weave in and out of her dreams. And then she felt his touch on her arm, steering her backwards through the crowd.

Unobtrusively they crept out of the wavering circle of torchlight, picking their way into the soft darkness of the tropical night. There was almost no moon, but Jake led the way, stepping as if by instinct along narrow pathways between the overhanging trees.

Amber followed him blindly, with complete trust. And then he stopped, and pulled her gently towards him.

'I love you, Amber. And I want to make love to you. Now. Tonight.'

She felt her tiredness drop from her, like a cloak. 'Jake, we can't! That bed—we'd rouse the whole village. We'll have to be patient...'

He shook his head. He was so very close...and she could feel his breath on her skin, warmer than the tropical night and softer than a caress.

'I have been patient, Amber. But not any longer. And besides, who needs a bed? We didn't need one before...'

As he spoke, Amber looked around and realised that, wherever they were going, it was not back to Ketut's compound. They had passed through the tall stone gates of the village and around them were the shadowy coconut groves, and the soft whispering sounds of the night.

Jake took her hand and drew her off into the velvet blackness beneath the trees. Amber could feel her pulse racing and a suffocating excitement rise in her throat at the knowledge of what was to come. And then, at the foot of a tall palm, they stopped. Jake turned her to face him, holding her hands in his. Her eyes were accustomed now, to the darkness. And his were like dark caverns, inviting her in.

'In Bali, before the Dutch came,' he said slowly, 'the women didn't hide their breasts. Remember the paintings we saw in Ubud? You looked beautiful tonight in that sarong, Amber. But now it's you I want to see.'

Uncertainly, her hands went to the fastening at her throat.

'No. Let me.' And she stood there, passively accepting, as his fingers felt in the dark for the tiny buttons, and undid each with careful delicacy. Until at last her blouse hung loose about her and, looking down, she could see the pale skin of her breasts gleam white in the darkness.

'Take it off, Amber.'

She shrugged her shoulders, and the silk slipped away, leaving her breasts bare and free above the sarong. The night air was cool on her overheated skin. And she felt a sudden liberation. This was what she had wanted, what she had waited for. Whether she knew it or not. Ever since that night in the glade, a month ago, she had been waiting...

No—longer than that. In some deep part of her she had been waiting since that first night, when he had set his seal on the lips of a child, and turned her into a woman. He had made her his own, then. And now he had come to claim her.

He was unknotting his sarong... And, Balinese style, she saw, he wore nothing beneath it. 'Jake,' she whispered, and her voice sounded strange and husky to her ears. She lifted her arms to draw him to her. 'Oh, Jake... I love you. I've wanted you so much.'

'And I love you.' His hands went to her waist, and she felt her sarong fall softly to join his at her feet. Only a wisp of cotton remained as a barrier between them. He knelt down, sliding her panties down her legs, and she stepped free of them. They were naked in the darkness. She knelt to join him.

And then his mouth met hers and she shut her eyes, and let him draw her down to lie with him on the soft, cool earth. And as he caressed her she felt the past and future meet and mend, arching seamlessly above them, as the coconuts merged with the trees in that other grove, and all the sensations she had felt there came flooding back.

But whereas, that last time, she had been moving in a dream, now she was wonderfully, miraculously awake. Every fibre, every nerve of her body seemed to sing with pleasure under his hands' touch. And her own fingers traced their pathways of delight across his damp-dewed skin, learning and relearning the lessons and responses of his flesh.

His body was above her now, a dark cloud against the darkness of the sky. And she could feel his urgency, matching it with a desire of her own, a passion that she had always known and always feared. But now she feared it no longer. It was a part of her; a part of him. And as their bodies joined, she arched against him. And cried out in joy.

CHAPTER TEN

AFTERWARDS, they lay still, his body covering her like a heavy blanket.

'Come along, my love,' he said at last. 'If we stay here, we'll fall asleep. And I'd hate Ketut to think we didn't like his bed.' Amber followed him, remembering that other awakening. But the pain of it was healed by the drugged pleasure that still pulsed through her heavy limbs. She felt that she was walking in a dream.

The chiming of the gamelan and the wailing chant of the puppet-master were still clearly audible in the still night air as they eased themselves gently on to the ancient mattress.

'Goodnight, Amber.' One hand lay gently, protectively, against her thigh. And within a few minutes she heard his breathing deepen into the gentle rhythm of sleep.

But to Amber sleep would not come. And as she lay there in the half-darkness, the thoughts which had hovered all day on the edge of her consciousness came crowding to the fore. Among them Jake's words. 'Surely you must have seen the notices...' And a memory, of Made pointing shyly at her stomach.

She had already been in Bali more than three weeks. And the signs in the temples had never applied to her... More than three weeks. Working

out the dates, that could only mean one thing.
That she was late.

But instead of panic she felt only a sense of
peace; of rightness. And a gratitude to her body
for keeping the secret until now. Until the right
time for her to know.

Because she did know. Her mind ran through
all the other possible reasons for the irregu-
larity—the stress of the last month; the exertion;
the change of scene. But she felt convinced they
were not the cause.

Somehow, Amber knew with absolute certainty that the reason was the most obvious one
of all.

She was carrying Jake's child.

She woke next morning with the same terrifying,
exhilarating thought. But with it came the beginnings of fear. After the pain which he had experienced in the past, what would Jake's reaction be
to the extra responsibilities of fatherhood, following on so soon after their marriage? She was
uneasily aware that she would have to pick the
right time for telling him.

Except that in the event the right time picked
itself. On the road back to the hotel, Ketut
stopped the *bemo* to pick up a group of young
women, as he had been used to doing with Amber
alone.

Amber glanced anxiously at Jake, to gauge his
reaction. There were six of them, all but one with
babies. Would he object?

But she soon realised that she needn't have
worried. Shifting more closely against her to

make room for the new arrivals, Jake grinned and said something in Indonesian. Whatever it was, it caused great hilarity among the women, and resulted in one mother handing over her plump little boy, fashionably dressed in a T-shirt and baseball cap but nothing else, for Jake to hold.

His inexperience was obvious, but so was his good-humoured willingness to learn. Even when a large and spreading damp patch testified to the infant's lack of bladder control, and sent its mother and her companions into renewed fits of giggles, Jake's smile hardly wavered.

'Isn't it supposed to wear nappies, or something?' he asked plaintively to Amber as he passed the child rather hastily back to its mother. 'Or at least give some kind of warning...?'

'Like a red light flashing on top of its head?' She tried to keep her voice light. 'You surprise me, Jake—I wouldn't have thought you were interested in babies.'

'I'm not sure I would have thought it, either, Mrs Farrell-to-be.' He grinned as he mopped his leg with a handkerchief. 'But it occurred to me that perhaps I ought to start getting my hand in. After all, we haven't exactly been taking any precautions... Fatherhood might strike at any moment.'

'Wrong tense.' The words were out before she could check them and then, having taken the plunge, she had to go on. 'Past tense, not future,' she explained, feeling the beginnings of desperation as he still said nothing. 'I realised last night,

Jake. I was trying to pluck up the courage to tell you. Do you mind?'

The pause before he spoke was agonisingly long, and Amber began to curse her impulsive revelation. She should have waited...

But then his words dispelled her doubts. 'If anything could make marrying you more perfect, that would be it,' he said softly. He reached out and touched her gently just below the waist of her sarong. 'But what about you, Amber? You don't feel...trapped?'

'Oh, no!' The relief was so great that she felt she was riding on air, combining with her tiredness to make her quite light-headed. 'Oh, Jake—I've always wanted children. Even before... And to have your baby——' She laughed delightedly and reached out to let one of the chubby babies clutch her finger. 'It was you I was worried about. But if you're pleased too... It's like a miracle. If it's a boy, I hope he's just like his father.'

But just for a second a shiver of uncertainty seemed to chill the happiness of her mood. A miracle... Everything had changed so quickly that it still didn't seem real. But then the fat little hand squeezed her finger, and the cloud lifted. This was real; this, and the life developing inside her.

She felt her heart swell with a joy that was almost too painful to contain. *'Anak cantik,'* she murmured. 'Beautiful baby.' And although the woman opposite looked pleased, it wasn't to her that Amber spoke.

*   *   *

The next few days seemed to slip by in a golden dream and, with only a single day of the holiday left, Amber realised that there was no time to do all they had planned.

'We never saw a cremation,' she said wistfully over breakfast. Jake had told her about the spectacular and exuberantly joyful ceremonies in which the Balinese freed the souls of their long-dead relations, but so far she had never seen one. 'And you were going to buy one of those paintings we saw in Ubud.'

'We could do that today,' Jake suggested.

But Amber shook her head. 'No, I can't. I promised I'd go with Made to the temple.' When he had heard their news, Ketut had been emphatic that the proper offerings ought to be made for the health and good fortune of the unborn child. 'I said I'd meet her this morning.'

'Then why don't you go with her to the temple and I'll go back to Ubud? It's a woman's ceremony, anyway—I'd only be in the way. I'll meet you back here this afternoon.'

It seemed the practical solution and so, despite her reluctance to be parted from Jake on their last day, Amber waved him goodbye in the rented car and waited for Ketut to collect her.

Made greeted her with shy delight and showed Amber how to make up the necessary offerings. On a base of intricately folded leaves, the various ingredients were piled with artistic care before being taken down to the temple and blessed by the priest.

The simple ceremony was unexpectedly moving, and Amber felt very close to the little

Balinese woman with her baby on her hip. All the differences in their lifestyle and heritage seemed to melt away, leaving just two women sharing the common experiences of their sex.

On their way out, in the outer courtyard, they met a group of women on their way in. One old woman seemed naggingly familiar—and then Amber realised why. It was the old woman who had given her her massage—and, looking more closely, she saw that the girl Wayan was also part of the group.

Her forgotten curiosity about that strange conversation with Jake came flooding back. In retrospect she was more certain than ever that his sudden departure had been caused by something the old lady had said. But what could it have been? Beckoning Made to stop, she resolved to find out.

Hoping that her companion's English would be sufficient to the task, she tried to explain as simply as possible what she wanted to know. And after initial puzzlement, Made managed to translate the question. But to Amber's surprise, the answer raised a smile.

'Your husband say no tell truth about baby,' Made translated laboriously.

Amber was bewildered. 'What do you mean? What baby?'

Now it was the other woman's turn to look bewildered. Obviously thinking it was her English that was at fault, she struggled to explain.

'When she say, you have baby, he say no.' She pointed at Amber's stomach for emphasis and laughed, as if she had made a joke.

'But how . . .? She couldn't have known about the baby then. Even I didn't know until a few days ago. You must have misunderstood.'

With another burst of giggles, Made translated this back into Balinese for the others—who seemed to find it as amusing as she did herself. Then she turned back to Amber.

'This woman, she——' She broke off, searching for a word, but failed to find it. 'When woman have baby, this old woman help her. This old woman see baby very soon. She always know. She see you have baby, she say to husband very fine baby. He not know?'

'No,' whispered Amber. 'No, he didn't know.' Somehow, the knowledge that Jake had been told about her pregnancy raised a cloud of panic in her brain. She wasn't sure why. It was hardly surprising that the news had come as a shock; and the fact that he had kept the news secret was surely a harmless enough deceit. Either he hadn't been sure whether to believe it, or he had been waiting for her to tell him herself.

There was nothing worrying in that. So why did she feel that some terrible knowledge was lurking just beneath the calm surface of her mind?

Amber suddenly realised that Made was looking at her in concern. Pulling herself together, she said goodbye to the midwife and her granddaughter and they headed back to where Ketut was waiting to drive them home.

The vague feeling of unease was still with her, but she pushed it aside, resolving not to mention the disturbing encounter to Jake. It was their last

day, after all. The end of their honeymoon...
Tomorrow it would all be over, and they would
be going back to England. To a new life. To
marriage...

And suddenly, it was all there. The whole story
was laid out in front of her, in letters a foot high.
She knew now why she had had that suffocating
feeling of panic at the old woman's revelations;
why she had instinctively avoided thinking it
through.

She hardly felt the jolting motion of the little
truck. Once she had seen it, Amber wondered
how she had failed to connect up the facts before.
Because the plain truth was that Jake had made
no mention of marriage before the old woman
had dropped her bombshell; had, after his initial
reaction, hardly even shown signs of more than
a friendly interest in her welfare.

But then the midwife's fingers had divined her
secret, and Jake had gone pale and rushed out
the room. And when he'd come back, everything
had changed. Within hours, he had turned their
relationship upside down. And she had never seen
the connection until now.

Bleakly, she thought through the whirlwind
events of the past few days. There had been her
uncle's letter—innocently warning Jake Farrell
that he was about to lose all he had gained by
shattering Amber's engagement to Simon. No
wonder Jake had kept its contents secret. He must
have been desperate...

And then, only hours later, the old midwife
had shown him a way out. A wife for the picking,
complete with child... But Jake had realised he

would have to move quickly. And so he had callously swept her away on a magic carpet of illusory passion. Even the fact that he wanted to marry by registrar's licence now made a terrible sense. Of course, he would have to make her his wife before she realised that his talk of renouncing his grandfather's legacy was just that—talk. Just lies. Like all the other lies that had betrayed her.

Once seen from the right angle, everything fell into place in a pattern of cold deliberation. The only thing that didn't fit was the fact that she loved him.

Amber sat there, staring out at the landscape, willing back the tears that burned at her eyelids and fighting for control. She mustn't let Made see. Jake mustn't find out that she knew. She couldn't bear to hear the lies again. And it wasn't safe. He could be so dangerously persuasive—even her uncle had been deceived.

And she would want so badly to believe him.

The plane was due to leave at eight the next morning. But by the time it finally took off two hours later the long delay had stretched Amber's nerves almost to breaking point.

And then, at last, they were airborne. But even then her waiting wasn't over. She had resolved to say nothing until the last long leg of the journey from Singapore—she couldn't take the risk that Jake might actually pull her off the plane. And he would have friends and contacts to call on, whereas she——

She would be more alone than ever. Her passport was in her handbag, returned to her at last, but Amber knew her companion too well to place much faith in such a flimsy guarantee. Only once the plane was directly *en route* for London would her freedom be assured.

Her freedom. The words had a gloomy, tearingly empty sound. What use was the freedom to be alone, to grieve, to burn up with frustrated love and desire for a man who deserved only hatred? To bring up a child whose every look, every gesture would remind her of its father——

But no, that was something she couldn't regret. If she couldn't have Jake, then at least she would have a living reminder of what they had shared. Of what she had thought they had shared... A piece of their common flesh, moulded into a child.

She had a momentary vision of a little boy, dark-haired and active, running towards her through the woods. And of dark eyes looking at her in love... Her own eyes filled with the tears that betrayal had not yet forced from her. And her mouth curved into a smile.

That would be better than any revenge.

As the minutes crawled by, Amber had to force herself to behave normally. She picked at the food, which seemed even more tasteless than normal, and hoped that her companion would put her subdued mood down to sorrow for the honeymoon that was ending.

But she needn't have worried. Jake himself seemed unusually distracted, and when she caught him looking at her it was with appraisal rather than concern. She realised that he must be on tenterhooks, wondering if this time his cruel gamble would pay off.

Amber found herself wondering what would happen if she gave in and let herself be swept along by his plans. If she could forget what she knew... And for a moment she was tempted. The last few days had given her a taste of what it might be to be Jake Farrell's wife. He had the power to evoke such passion; to carry her into another world...

Because she loved him. Whatever happened, whatever lies he had told, that was the inescapable truth. She loved Jake Farrell, and he was the father of her child. So why couldn't she put her knowledge behind her, and accept the life he was offering her? He might not love her, but he would be kind. It would be in his interest to treat her well. And perhaps...

Perhaps... Amber remembered his words over dinner on the night of his arrival in Bali. 'Good and evil are two sides of the same coin; and most people are a mixture of the two...' Was it possible that the love he had faked might take root and grow? She remembered the things he had said; the way he had looked. It couldn't all have been lies...

But although her heartbeat quickened at the thought Amber forced herself to push it away. She should be comforting herself with the knowledge that, financially at least, she was perfectly capable of bringing up a child by herself, not swaying herself with false hopes.

When once you ignored his traitorous lies, Jake Farrell's actions spoke louder than any words. And what they spoke of was betrayal.

Jakarta passed; then Singapore. And still Amber waited. Telling him seemed suddenly as difficult as her previous silence. And she convinced herself that it would be stupid to speak too early; Jake would only try and argue her out of her decision.

So she dozed fitfully, and read, and tried to marshal her arguments. Knowing all the time that when she told him it wouldn't be arguments that mattered. It would be the conviction with which she could gaze into those eyes. And tell that one, central lie.

Not until most of a long day had dragged painfully by did she take the plunge, just a few hours from their touchdown at Heathrow airport.

'Jake, I've got something to tell you.'

Something in her desperate tone obviously signalled the gravity of what she was trying to say and he looked at her warily.

'What is it, Tiger-eyes?'

His use of the old nickname cut like a knife, but she forced herself to go on. 'Jake, I know why you're doing this,' she said bluntly. There, it was out now... 'The wedding, I mean. And I'm not going through with it. You don't love me, and I won't make do with less. Ironic, isn't it? It was you who taught me that.'

He was staring at her as if she had gone mad. 'What the hell do you mean—you know why I'm doing this? I wasn't aware there was any secret about it. It's all quite simple. I love you, you love

me, and we're going to be married as soon as we
get back to England.'

'No!' The almost wordless cry hung in the air
between them. 'No, Jake—I won't. You don't
really love me. You want a wife and a child—
and there I was, all ready and waiting. I can see
why you were tempted. I'm not even sure I blame
you. But it's no good now, Jake. You see,
I know——'

She was gabbling now, the words spilling out
so fast that she hardly knew what she was saying.
'We'll be all right, the baby and I. I've got my
own income from Grandfather Matthew's will,
remember?'

'I remember that you said you loved me,
Amber.' There was real hurt on his face, and she
felt herself wavering. But then she had known he
would be persuasive. She had to be strong... His
voice went on, hammering at the gates she had
closed in her mind. 'And besides, woman, you're
raving. It may have escaped your memory, but
you didn't tell me about the baby until after I
proposed. If I was that cold-blooded, I'd hardly
buy a pig in a poke.'

He looked challengingly at her, but Amber held
her gaze steady. 'But you knew already, Jake.' It
was a statement, not a question. And she saw his
eyes shift momentarily, admitting his deceit.
'That old woman; the masseuse—she told you.
I met her again at the temple and Made translated.' She paused, to let her words sink in, then
added bitterly, 'That was why you rushed off that
day, wasn't it? You had to decide what to do.'

And, remembering his face then, she felt almost sorry for him. Perhaps it hadn't been such an easy decision—perhaps it hadn't been as cold-blooded as she had imagined. But, in the end, he had chosen betrayal...

Jake shrugged and pulled her round to face him. 'All right—so I admit it.' He shook her gently. 'I knew about the baby. But you're wrong if you think that's why I asked you to marry me, Amber. I love——'

'Don't say it. Please. I won't believe you. And it only makes this harder.' She looked Jake fiercely in the eyes. 'I don't know whether you planned it from the beginning. Perhaps all you wanted was to make sure there was no chance of a reconciliation between me and Simon. Did you think then he might agree to share the money? But then you saw a chance to take it all.'

'No, damn you! No! It wasn't—Amber, I swear——'

'Then swear to this, Jake. Tell me the truth. If you hadn't found out about the baby, would you have proposed to me when you did?'

He held her gaze for a moment, then slumped back into his seat. 'For God's sake.' He sounded tired beyond the weariness of the journey, and Amber, despite herself, felt her heart go out to him. But she had to be strong...

'This is hardly the ideal time to discuss this,' he went on, bleakly. 'But no, if you want the truth, I wouldn't. Not then. I wanted——'

'What did you want? No—don't bother to answer.' Amber knew that it was time to put an end to the discussion. The longer he talked, the more she would waver. And she owed it to both of them to make the break as clean as possible.

'I wouldn't believe you, Jake. Whatever you said.' She shook her head angrily. 'And besides——'

This was it now. The one big lie. 'I don't love you, Jake.' Somehow, she forced the words out. 'I can't deny that we're physically attracted, but that's no basis for a marriage. When I thought you at least cared for me, I thought I could go through with it for the baby's sake, but now I realise that I can't. You've been there before, Jake—you ought to know.'

His face was changing as she spoke and Amber was almost afraid of the bitter, contemptuous light that shone in his eyes. But it had to be said. As long as he knew she was vulnerable, she would never be safe from him.

When he spoke, his voice was dangerously low. 'Are you saying that you don't love me, Amber? That you never loved me?'

She heard the answer as if in someone else's voice. 'Yes, Jake—that's exactly what I'm saying.' The one central lie...

'Then God damn you to hell!' And as his control finally broke Amber could hear the rustling as the other passengers turned round to stare at the drama in their midst. But Jake was oblivious. He stormed down the aisle, and she could hear his raised voice demanding a new seat from the stewardess.

So that was it. It was finished. And, staring at the blank back of the seat in front of her, Amber wondered how long it would be before the searing pain of loss diminished to a bearable ache.

CHAPTER ELEVEN

IN THE International Arrivals section of Heathrow Terminal Four, Amber stood waiting for her luggage to appear on the carousel. All she had seen of Jake since he had stormed away on the plane was a brief glimpse of his back in the crowd some distance in front of her.

Now she stood self-effacingly, head down, eyes fixed on the slowly moving belt. She knew that it would be more than she could bear to catch his eye accidentally, and have to face the cutting contempt in his gaze.

It had been the only way. She knew that. So long as he believed that she cared for him, he would have gone on trying to talk her round. And what did it matter what he thought of her? But that didn't make it any easier to bear.

Dazed with tiredness and grief, Amber didn't notice her case until it was right in front of her. With a gasp, she made a grab for it, only to be forestalled by an arm that reached from behind to pluck it off the conveyor as if it were empty, instead of packed with twice as much as had filled it on the way out.

'Oh, thank you——' she began. Then she realised that she recognised that arm only too well.

'I'll give you a lift home,' Jake said curtly. 'My car's parked here, and it's the least I can do.'

Amber started to object, but he was already striding towards Customs with a case in each hand, ignoring the trolley she had reserved. He walked so fast, as if propelled by his anger, that she had to half run to keep up with him.

'There's no need, Jake,' she protested weakly. If only she weren't so tired . . . 'I was planning to go home by train.'

'Where to? It may have slipped your memory, but thanks to me you're *persona non grata* with our dear aunt. She's a stubborn old woman, Amber. What if she decides to show you the door?'

'Then I'll stay with Sandra, if she'll have me.' The thought made her feel decidedly uncomfortable, but sooner or later she would have to find out where she stood with her friend. And whether there was any truth in Jake's theory about her and Simon . . . 'Or at the Red Lion,' she went on. 'I'm not helpless, Jake. I——'

'Look,' he broke in wearily, 'all I'm offering is a lift. If not back to Marchings, then at least up to London, to the station. You can phone your uncle from there and find out what the reception is likely to be. OK?'

She hesitated a moment, and he pressed home his point. 'You're in no state to start battling with the Tube with all that luggage, Tiger-eyes. Whatever happens, I'm still the father of that child and you might as well get used to accepting help from me. Because, like it or not, you're going to get a lot of practice.'

'But I don't want——'

But this time he turned on her with a snarl that was almost animal. 'I don't give a damn what you want, Amber. You're exhausted and you're pregnant with my child. And you're coming with me.'

By then, Amber's stock of resistance was used up, and she found herself following him obediently out to his car. But almost as soon as they turned out of the airport she realised that something was wrong.

'Jake, I thought you were driving me to the station? This is the wrong way...' But he ignored her and just kept driving. Amber bit her lip. What was he up to—and why did he have to make it all so difficult? The last thing she wanted was to be trapped in the car with him all the way back to Marchings. But he couldn't force her. He would have to pull up at one of the many sets of traffic-lights, and then——

As if he had read her thoughts, Jake cut in roughly, 'The doors are centrally locked, so don't try anything stupid. Don't worry, you little fool, I'm not kidnapping you. I'm just taking you on a visit.'

'A visit where?'

For a long time, he didn't answer. And, seeing his dark, forbidding face, she didn't dare repeat the question. But then they cleared the suburbs, and Jake swung the car out on to the motorway. And spoke with a savage emphasis.

'Back to the place where all this started, Tiger-eyes. Because if ever you needed a thinking-place then now's the time.'

*   *   *

It was midday before they reached the glade, Jake, silent and furious, half dragging her up the steep path through the woods. 'I don't know why you're doing this.' Amber reached down to staunch a trickle of blood that ran down one leg where the brambles had torn her skin. 'It won't change anything.'

'Won't it?' His voice was different now, still harsh, but full of meaning. 'I wouldn't be so sure. Some places have power—the Balinese know that. This is the third time we've been here, Amber. And twice before our lives have changed.'

Twice before? What did he mean? But she knew what he meant—for her at least. The frail, scented memory of that first meeting stood for her as the pivot between child and adult. When his lips had touched hers, it had opened a gateway... And she had stepped through it into the fires of life.

But for him? What could it have meant to him, an hour spent with a child? It was just more lies—another trick to betray her.

'I won't listen, Jake.' She held her hands to her ears, childish in her desperation. 'I don't want to hear any more——'

'I told you—I don't give a damn what you want, Amber. Like it or not, you're going to hear my side of the story. Then, if you want to go, you can. But not before.'

'You can't make me...' But her voice petered out. If there was one thing she had learned about Jake Farrell, it was that he could make her... He could make her do almost anything he wanted.

Except marry him. The thought gave her something to cling to. 'Go on, then.' She crossed her arms and stared up at him defiantly. 'But since you admitted in the plane that you only asked me to marry you because you knew about the baby I find it hard to imagine what you're going to say.' She felt quite pleased with her calm, mocking tone. 'That was rather careless of you, Jake. But I suppose you were taken by surprise.'

'Shut up and listen, Amber.' His voice was calmer now, but forceful. 'What I said in the plane was true enough. But you didn't let me finish. I hadn't planned to ask you then—but I knew damn well that I would marry you eventually. You don't think I went through all this just to let you get away from me again?'

Amber could scarcely believe what she was hearing. '*You* go through all this? What about me? You break up my wedding, then barge in on my honeymoon as if——'

'I told you to shut up and listen.' There was something in him that commanded obedience, and she found herself subsiding reluctantly into silence. 'I know you've been through a lot,' he went on more gently. 'In fact, that's exactly my point, Tiger-eyes. I was determined to take things slowly and quietly, and not risk scaring you off. You were just beginning to trust me, but I knew perfectly well that it was a fragile sort of trust. I was treading on eggshells, trying not to disturb it, and I was convinced that if I once mentioned marriage, or gave you the slightest hint of it, you'd be bound to get it into your head that I was still a contender for Grandfather's money.'

'Oh, so you admit that did occur to you?' That was better. She had to keep that edge of anger. It was the only protection she had...

'Occur to me?' The words seemed to burst from him. 'Amber, after what had already happened I could hardly think of anything else. Why else do you think I kept my hands off you for so long? I was planning to leave it until we got back, and I could get a proper agreement drawn up with Simon, renouncing my claim. That's why the old crone's news knocked the wind out of me. I suddenly realised that I didn't have that sort of time. At any moment, you might realise——'

'Realise what, Jake? That it wasn't me you were really interested in?'

'No.' His voice sounded flat now, as if he were reining it in. 'That you were pregnant. I'd been through that once with Vicky, remember. I'd seen how terrified she felt; how alone. I didn't ever want that to happen to you. If you were having my child, I wanted it to be a joyful discovery— but, thanks to me, you didn't even have your family to run to. I wanted to protect you...' His face showed the strain of emotion now, his lean features looking almost haggard. Amber felt a flicker of belief stir in her, before she could quell it. And as if he had sensed it she saw him relax. 'So, yes, I did step things up a bit.' His mouth twisted wryly. 'But that doesn't mean——'

'Stepped things up a bit! Up to then, you'd never shown the slightest——' Amber heard her voice hit a new pitch of indignation, her momentary sympathy forgotten. 'In fact you made it quite obvious that you were more interested in that girl on the beach than in me. And now you have the cheek——'

But Jake shook his head. 'Don't grudge me that, Tiger-eyes. Have you any idea what I was going through on the beach every day, doing my "Uncle Jake" act; helping you with your sun-oil and trying not to ravish you there and then on the sand? It was hell—though it was almost worth it to see how much it annoyed you.'

He grinned and carried on before she could disentangle her retort from her tongue. 'If it hadn't been for Wayan's taking my mind off things I don't know how I'd have coped.' A glint of wickedness came into his eyes. 'I had a feeling that you were getting quite jealous of Wayan.'

'Oh—that's ridiculous!' To her horror, Amber felt a deep blush spread over her face. 'Of course I wasn't—I wouldn't——' She stopped in frustrated incoherence. Why was it that she didn't seem able to finish a sentence any more?

But Jake only grinned. 'Although in fact I spent most of my time talking to her about you. But she was a useful distraction. My plan was to give you the holiday as a breathing space and then, when we came back, to offer you a job at Person to Person. You were ideally qualified, after all, and that would have made sure we kept in contact. I just hoped we'd go on from there.' He paused. 'I was prepared to wait, Amber. After all, I'd waited long enough. But I wasn't going to let you go again.'

Again? The word seemed to echo through her head. What did he mean, again? Amber walked slowly across the clearing towards the old oak, her mind awhirl. If what he said was true ... But could she believe him? His words had the ring of truth, but even so ... There was still so much that Jake Farrell hadn't explained. Only somehow, with his voice caressing her ears, it was hard to remember not to trust him.

But he was speaking again, urging her. 'You must believe me, Amber. I told you the truth, that day in the monkey-forest at Ubud. I don't want old Farrell's money. No one should be tempted to make the most important decision of their life on those sort of grounds. When we go back, you can ask your uncle. I told him what I planned to do.'

Of course; the letter. That was something else he hadn't explained. 'I know you fooled my uncle,' she said unsteadily. 'He told you where I was, didn't he? I thought it was Sandra, but it was Uncle Bob. He wrote you a letter, but you didn't tell me about it. Why not, Jake?' It was a cry from the heart, and, hearing it, Amber knew with sick certainty that she was on the verge of succumbing to the lies she wanted so badly to believe. 'Why didn't you tell me about the letter?'

'What?' Jake seemed genuinely taken aback. 'What's that got to do with it, Tiger-eyes? And how did you know——?'

'Oh, don't pretend. I saw the letter, Jake. I read it. My uncle told you that Simon and Sandra were in love. That they might get married. No wonder you were so keen to speed up your plans.'

To her amazement, he actually laughed. 'Oh, my poor Amber. What a tangle you've made for yourself! I kept that letter quiet for the simple reason that I didn't want to risk hurting you. You seemed to be getting over Simon, but I wasn't at all sure you were ready to cope with the news that he was consoling himself in the arms of your best friend. And besides, if you have read the letter, then you ought to remember that that particular piece of news didn't exactly come as a shock to me. I was expecting it—your uncle just confirmed my suspicions.'

'But how could you know? I mean, I know them both well, Jake, and I never——'

He shrugged. 'Oh, a combination of things. Maybe you were too close to see it. But that other summer—they were very close, you know. Close enough for our darling aunt to spot that her son was in danger of falling for the housekeeper's daughter and whisk the temptation off to secretarial college. Or did you think that was just her natural generosity shining through? So, naturally, you and Simon were thrown together. Much more suitable. But in the church——' Jake's voice suddenly became sombre. 'I'm sorry, Amber. But it was her he ran to. Not to you.'

Amber stared at him, the pieces locking together in her memory. 'I suppose you might be right,' she said slowly. 'But you didn't need to worry. If it is true...I'd be pleased, more than anything. For both of them.'

Jake breathed a sigh of relief. 'Thank God for that. You were so quiet coming over that I was afraid you were moping about Simon—that coming back had reminded you...'

So that had been it; so simple. And by the very force of his simplicity Amber found herself believing him. She felt the last of her defences peel away. 'I've hardly thought of him,' she admitted. 'Does that sound awful? Poor Simon...'

But Jake shook his head. 'No,' he said gently. 'Lucky Simon. And lucky me. Not everyone gets a second chance at love.'

A second chance... And then his words came floating back to her. 'This is the third time we've been here, Amber. And twice before, our lives have changed... I wasn't going to let you go again...' She almost held her breath, looking up at him. 'A second chance?'

And they both knew she wasn't talking about Simon. 'The last time I came here, Amber, I was doing the same as you,' he said seriously. 'Remembering. I drove down for the wedding, but once I got as far as the Hall I couldn't face it. So I decided to come up here. To the place where it all started. I don't know what I expected to happen. But the past came back to life.'

Amber found herself whispering. 'Jake, what do you mean?'

But he was looking at her with eyes that seemed to gaze down through the years. 'I mean that I loved you, Amber. From the first time I saw you here. From the first time I touched you...'

She shook her head as if to clear it from the daze of hope that suddenly afflicted her. 'But I was only a child, Jake. You can't expect me to believe——'

'That a man of twenty-four could fall in love with a flame-haired wood-nymph of fifteen? No,

I wouldn't expect you to believe it. I didn't quite believe in it myself. It was impossible; ridiculous. Even disgraceful. And so I went away, to let you do your growing-up. For a while, I even thought that I'd forgotten. And then one morning I was reading *The Times*, and I saw the notice of your engagement to Simon. And I discovered that I hadn't forgotten my wood-nymph after all.'

'My engagement! But that was three years ago—my first term at university. Why did you wait so long?' Somehow, without noticing the transition, she had stopped fighting her tremulous belief. 'Oh, Jake—why did you wait?'

'What could I do?' His mouth quirked in a wry smile. 'I thought you loved him, remember. You'd made your choice—I could hardly turn up on the doorstep and forbid the banns. And besides, it all seemed like a dream by then, even to me. I thought you'd have forgotten altogether.'

'I had, until I saw you again. You should have come back, Jake. I would have remembered...'

He shook his head. 'Would you? Or would it have been just the same? And it was too late, almost immediately. Just after that, old Matthew died and I decided to do my well-known impression of a man tying his life in a grannyknot.'

He gave a wry smile. 'In fact, I blame you for that, Tiger-eyes—at least partially. Losing a wood-nymph is apt to make a man cynical. Besides, I did come back. And you were here...' His voice too was soft, and she could barely hear it over the murmur of the trees. 'Only this time you weren't a child, Amber. My wood-nymph had grown up. I wasn't sure then whether I loved you or hated you. But I couldn't resist you. And then in the morning I woke up and found you gone.'

'I was afraid.' And saying it, Amber realised that the fear had been with her ever since. But now, back in the grove, it had melted away. 'I was so scared of being like my mother.'

'Poor Aunt Claudine.' Jake smiled. 'I remember her quite well, you know. She used to descend on my parents occasionally, when she had nowhere else to go. I remember her as being much larger than life—everything was exaggerated to her; either black or white.'

Amber felt his breath on her face as he took a step closer. 'Where she went wrong, my love, was in not realising that passion isn't the end of the story. That it's just the beginning...'

And then there was only a swelling conviction that everything would be all right, that this time the man in the glade would be her lover. And not a demon...

But Jake was speaking again, and his voice was full of remorse. 'I should have realised what you were going through, Amber; I should have been strong for you; forced your hand. You tried to tell me. But I was still balanced between loving you and hating you for making me love you. And when you didn't turn up to meet me...'

'How long did you wait?'

He gave a half-smile, remembering. 'All night. I'd brought a flask of brandy with me and I ended up drinking so much of it to keep warm that if you had turned up *you'd* have had to drive us out of here. But by then I think I knew you weren't coming. I hated you then, Amber. Or thought I did. So I kept drinking to try and dull the pain.'

'You hid it well, in the church. But I knew.'

'What I did in the church was unforgivable.'

'Not unforgivable, Jake. It hurt, but it saved my life. Like surgery. I can't believe, now, what I was going to do.'

'I should have come back earlier, Tiger-eyes. I should have looked after you.'

He held out his hand and she moved, unthinking, to take it. And then he looked down at her, and his eyes seemed suddenly to darken. 'Say it here, Amber, and I'll believe you. Tell me you don't love me.'

She opened her mouth, but the words seemed to stick in her throat.

'I can't.'

'Then tell me you do.'

She looked back at him, and the whole world seemed to swirl away into those dark, demanding eyes. And there were no longer any questions, but only answers. Only one answer, to all the questions in the world.

'I love you, Jake.'

He sighed, as if the breath would leave his body. And pulled her into his arms. They stood there, listening to the leaves rustling overhead. Until at last he spoke.

'I want to marry you soon, my darling. I won't feel safe until I do. I'll keep feeling that my wood-nymph might somehow spirit herself away.' And, looking down at her, he smiled with a tenderness that made her bones shiver. 'That's why I wanted to marry by registrar's licence—though I dare say you managed to convince yourself that it was all part of some nefarious scheme. But if you prefer we could wait for the banns and marry in church. I just want to make sure that you're really and finally mine.'

It should have set the seal on her happiness. But instead, Amber looked down, her joy tarnished by a scratching of discomfort. 'Yes...'

'What's the matter, Tiger-eyes?' Jake's tone roughened again. 'Don't tell me you still don't believe me?'

She rushed to reassure him. 'Oh, no—I do. Of course I do. It's just... I don't know. Only a register office seems somehow unromantic. But on the other hand I'm not sure I could go through another church wedding—not so soon. It would bring it all back. Oh, Jake—I'm sorry. I'm being very silly.'

'You're not being silly, poor darling,' he said, gently again now. 'I should have thought... But there's a simple enough solution. We'll go back to Bali and get married there. I'll get Ketut to arrange it. He'll be delighted.'

'Back to Bali! But what will they think...?' She flushed. 'Jake, they think we're married already. And they know about the baby...'

But he only smiled. 'Don't worry about it, Tiger-eyes. The traditional form of marriage in Bali is so complex and expensive that most young men just kidnap their bride and carry her off for an unofficial honeymoon. The wedding ceremony has to wait until they get back.'

He grinned more broadly. 'So you see, my hijacking your honeymoon is in the best Balinese tradition. Ketut and Made won't blink an eye. And a Balinese wedding is quite something. The actual ceremony is quite simple—just passing a flower between us, and a blessing from the priest. But the party can go on for up to twenty days and nights.'

He paused, then added seriously, 'But whatever we do, Amber, that won't be our real wedding. I married you here in the glade, a month ago. Anything else will be just a celebration.'

'Oh, Jake...' She felt the tears start in her eyes again, but this time they were tears of pure joy. 'Oh, Jake—that would be lovely. I do love you... I can't tell you how much.'

Gently, he kissed the wetness from her cheeks. 'You already have, Amber. But you can tell me again. As often as you like. That half-hour on the plane, before I realised that you must be lying—they were the worst thirty minutes of my life.'

'Only half an hour?' She felt almost affronted, remembering the hours of misery she had suffered. 'How did you realise so quickly?'

'Because when I'd calmed down I realised that whatever you said I already knew that you loved me. That night at the *odalan*—nothing could have been as perfect as that if it was built on a lie.' His brow creased a little. 'You should have known that, Amber. But then wood-nymphs were never famous for their logic.'

As if to illustrate, he let his hands run down her spine, and smiled in triumph at her shiver of response. 'You see? Your body knows much better—and I decided that's what I would trust.'

And then he was crushing her, hugging her to him. 'But don't ever do that to me again, Tiger-eyes. From now on, I only want the truth. That you love me. That you're going to marry me. And that you're going to have our baby...'

Above them, a gust of wind rippled the trees, as if the glade itself was murmuring its assent. And Amber felt a surge of purest joy. Suddenly everything seemed to fit together, all the pain and unhappiness of the last month dropping effortlessly into place in a much wider pattern. A pattern of happiness...

And now that pattern was complete. Jake Farrell had set out to hijack her honeymoon. But he had ended by stealing her heart.

POSTCARDS FROM EUROPE

HARLEQUIN PRESENTS®

Hi—

I'm in trouble—I'm
engaged to Stuart, but I
suddenly wish my rela-
tionship with Jan Breydel
wasn't strictly business.
Perhaps it's simply the
fairy-tale setting of
Bruges. Belgium is such a
romantic country!

Love, Geraldine

Travel across Europe in 1994 with Harlequin
Presents. Collect a new Postcards From
Europe title each month!

Don't miss
THE BRUGES ENGAGEMENT
by Madeleine Ker
Harlequin Presents #1650

Available in May, wherever
Harlequin Presents books are sold.

HPPFE5

HARLEQUIN®

Don't miss these Harlequin favorites by some of our most distinguished authors!
And now, you can receive a discount by ordering two or more titles!

HT #25551	THE OTHER WOMAN by Candace Schuler	$2.99	☐
HT #25539	FOOLS RUSH IN by Vicki Lewis Thompson	$2.99	☐
HP #11550	THE GOLDEN GREEK by Sally Wentworth	$2.89	☐
HP #11603	PAST ALL REASON by Kay Thorpe	$2.99	☐
HR #03228	MEANT FOR EACH OTHER by Rebecca Winters	$2.89	☐
HR #03268	THE BAD PENNY by Susan Fox	$2.99	☐
HS #70532	TOUCH THE DAWN by Karen Young	$3.39	☐
HS #70540	FOR THE LOVE OF IVY by Barbara Kaye	$3.39	☐
HI #22177	MINDGAME by Laura Pender	$2.79	☐
HI #22214	TO DIE FOR by M.J. Rodgers	$2.89	☐
HAR #16421	HAPPY NEW YEAR, DARLING by Margaret St. George	$3.29	☐
HAR #16507	THE UNEXPECTED GROOM by Muriel Jensen	$3.50	☐
HH #28774	SPINDRIFT by Miranda Jarrett	$3.99	☐
HH #28782	SWEET SENSATIONS by Julie Tetel	$3.99	☐

Harlequin Promotional Titles

#83259	UNTAMED MAVERICK HEARTS	$4.99	☐
	(Short-story collection featuring Heather Graham Pozzessere, Patricia Potter, Joan Johnston)		

(limited quantities available on certain titles)

	AMOUNT	$
DEDUCT:	10% DISCOUNT FOR 2+ BOOKS	$
	POSTAGE & HANDLING	$
	($1.00 for one book, 50¢ for each additional)	
	APPLICABLE TAXES*	$ _____
	TOTAL PAYABLE	$ _____
	(check or money order—please do not send cash)	

To order, complete this form and send it, along with a check or money order for the total above, payable to Harlequin Books, to: **In the U.S.:** 3010 Walden Avenue, P.O. Box 9047, Buffalo, NY 14269-9047; **In Canada:** P.O. Box 613, Fort Erie, Ontario, L2A 5X3.

Name: _____

Address: _____ City: _____

State/Prov.: _____ Zip/Postal Code: _____

*New York residents remit applicable sales taxes.
 Canadian residents remit applicable GST and provincial taxes.

Travel across Europe in 1994
with Harlequin Presents and...

As you travel across Europe in 1994, visiting your favorite countries with your favorite authors, don't forget to collect four proofs of purchase to redeem for an appealing photo album. This photo album can hold over fifty 4"×6" pictures of your travels and will be a precious keepsake in the years to come!

One proof of purchase can be found in the back pages of each POSTCARDS FROM EUROPE title...one every month until December 1994.

To receive your gift, please fill out the information below and mail four (4) original proof-of-purchase coupons from any Harlequin Presents POSTCARDS FROM EUROPE title plus $3.00 for postage and handling (check or money order—do not send cash), payable to Harlequin Books, to: IN THE U.S.: P.O. Box 9048, Buffalo, NY, 14269-9048; IN CANADA: P.O. Box 623, Fort Erie, Ontario, L2A 5X3.

Requests must be received by January 31, 1995.
Please allow 4–6 weeks after receipt of order for delivery.

Name: _____
Address: _____
_____
City: _____
State/Province: _____
Zip/Postal Code: _____
Account No: _____
ONE PROOF OF PURCHASE   077 KBY